Josephine AGAINST THE Sea

Josephine AGAINST THE Sea

WITHDRAWN

SHAKIRAH BOURNE

Scholastic Press / New York

All rights reserved. Published by Scholastic Press, an imprint of Scholastic Inc., *Publishers since 1920*. SCHOLASTIC, SCHOLASTIC PRESS, and associated logos are trademarks and/or registered trademarks of Scholastic Inc.

Library of Congress Cataloging-in-Publication Data available

ISBN 978-1-338-64208-7

1 2021

Printed in the U.S.A.   23

First edition, July 2021

Book design by Keirsten Geise

To children who stare at the sea, wondering what lies beneath.
To the Caribbean ancestors who refused to let our stories die.

CHAPTER 1

It's 4:58 p.m. and Daddy still isn't back from his date. I should have never allowed him to leave home.

He's been gone for two whole hours. Two hours we could have spent watching the cricket match on TV! But nooo, he *had* to go out and have ice cream with "a friend." We have good cherry-vanilla ice cream right here in the freezer. He could have eaten that with me.

With my binoculars, I see Jalopy, his old white Jeep, coming from at least two minutes away. I yank the binoculars away from my face and glance at the old brass clock.

4:59 p.m.

He promised to be back by five.

He's officially going to be late.

I peer through the binoculars again and notice a woman with big, curly hair in the passenger seat. *And he's not alone.*

I growl under my breath and prepare to defend my territory. Across the street, I notice Ahkai, my neighbor and best friend, taking out the garbage. His face is almost as sour as mine.

I can guess what's in that bag. It's Saturday, which means his mother's made steamed flying fish and corn-meal cou-cou for his entire family.

That's when an idea hits me.

Operation Slime!

I'm going to make sure that "friend" gets a small taste of life with a fisherman like my daddy. I do my evil laugh—it starts with a low chuckle and climbs into a roaring cackle.

Ahkai looks up at my window, shakes his head, and hurries back inside.

He knows what's coming...

I scramble to message him from my walkie-talkie under the bed.

"Come in, Ahkai. Over."

I let go of the button and wait.

Just static.

The old brass clock ticks.

"Ahkai, youuu better ANSWER ME! Over."

Silence.

Oh, right. I forgot Ahkai insists on using code names.

"Come in, Alpha Mike. Over."

Static, and then—

"This is Alpha Mike. Alpha Mike. Alpha Mike . . ." I wait for Ahkai to finish whispering his code name exactly five times. That's just how he is. He's on the— what's it called again? It reminds me of something wonderful . . . Awesome? Rhythm? Autism! That's it. He's on the autism spectrum, and I am one of the few people Ahkai utters a word to.

People think he's odd, but I don't mind. He's my best friend in the whole world. Actually, he's my only friend in the whole world, which is fine by me.

"Alpha Mike, retrieve the stinky garbage and bring it to my location. Over."

I waste precious seconds trying to persuade Ahkai to hide in the hibiscus bushes. I don't know why he bothers to protest. He never turns his back on a mission.

Though the bush is about four feet high, it completely covers his short, slight frame. He's dressed the part of a good lookout, wearing a dark green shirt and black jeans. I push a red hibiscus flower into the black knitted tam on his head to make sure he's fully camouflaged.

Then, I hear a jackhammer rattling in the distance. That's Jalopy, coughing its way home. I really didn't need binoculars—I can hear that engine coming from a mile away. I rush inside to get into position at the top of the stairs.

Soon, Ahkai chimes in on the walkie-talkie.

"The target has left the rickety vehicle. She is approaching the red *Hibiscus furcellatus* bush and ascending the stairs. She will reach your location in approximately ten point three seconds. Nine point six seconds. Eight—"

I put the walkie-talkie on the floor and pick up my battered cricket ball. Since "the incident," I'm not allowed near Coach Broomes's equipment room, so I'm forced to hunt for rejected cricket balls like some kind of cow-leather scavenger. I had fished this one out of the bushes when Jared, the best cricket player at my school, hit it for six. Almost all the thread is gone, and I get little bounce when it hits the grass. But I don't need bounce now; I need precision.

The bucket of slime on top of the fridge has to tip at just the right angle.

I grip the cricket ball between two fingers for a

straight throw. I've heard people on TV compare cricket to baseball because both sports use bats, but cricket is FAR superior. For one thing, cricket balls are much harder and heavier, which will come in handy to move the full bucket.

Focus. Precision. Speed.

Every good bowler knows the best type of delivery to hit the target, and unfortunately for Daddy's date, I'm the best bowler in the village.

The back door opens, and I know my daddy—the gentleman that he is—will let his "friend" inside the house first. I am overwhelmed by the smell of fruity, cheap perfume.

Now!

I release the ball and watch as it speeds toward the target.

Yes! Yes!

Nooo . . .

The ball misses the rim of the bucket by a whisper. I hope that its wind is enough to make the bucket lose balance from the edge of the refrigerator, but it's not my lucky day. Instead, the ball continues across the kitchen and crashes through the window.

The glass shatters.

Daddy's date screams and tries to duck, but she's

wobbly on her six-inch heels. Daddy grabs her by the arm, steadying her. He looks at the broken glass on the floor, and then glares at me.

"Josephine Elisabeth Zara Cadogan!"

Through the open door I see Ahkai diving from the hibiscus bushes, scrambling to get away before he's discovered. As usual, he trips over his two left feet, decides to stay on the ground, and crawls through the gate next door.

"'Ow much times I must tell you not to throw balls in the 'ouse!" Daddy slaps the side of the fridge in frustration.

I gasp as the bucket rocks. Daddy glances up and manages to jump out of the way just before the bucket tips over.

I guess it's my lucky day after all.

All the contents—the fish guts and scales—fall on Daddy's date. It looks like a brain has exploded on top of her head, with one particularly long, fat piece of entrails sliding down her ear and plopping onto her bare shoulder like a vomit-colored earthworm. I can't help but gag at the putrid smell of the fish intestines. A swarm of flies zips through the back door and dances above her head, eager to feast on the foul, rotting flesh.

"Omigod omigod omigod!" she cries.

With a trembling hand, she plucks a fish head from her bouncy hair. A long string of slime clings to her fingers. It reminds me of the gooey trail a slug leaves behind when trying to escape a salt ambush.

"This is too much! I just can't!" she yells. Daddy's date yanks the hair off her head, exposing cornrows covered by a tan stocking cap. She throws the curly brown wig on the ground and heads for the door.

"Debbie! Wait—" Daddy calls after her, but she ignores him.

Goodbye, "friend."

Daddy turns around right in time to see the smug look on my face.

Uh-oh.

CHAPTER 2

Daddy can't ground me if he can't catch me!

I race to my bedroom, but Daddy's long legs stride up the stairs behind me, three or four at a time. I got my height from Daddy. I'm already taller than all the boys in my class, and really skinny—like a string bean.

Daddy must be hopping mad because he's forgotten about his bad knee. At least twice a week I have to rub it with Benjie's Balm, a strong vapor rub that helps with the pain.

I burst into my room and try to shut the door, but Daddy's already pushing against it, trying to force his way inside. It's a losing battle—eighty pounds versus two-ten, but I don't give up. There is only one day left of summer vacation and I don't want to spend it staring at the ceiling in my room.

"It's not my fault! It was an accident! You is the one who knock down the bucket!" I yell, trying to muster superhuman strength. But I know my excuses are as pointless as my attempt to block the door.

I move my body away, and Daddy stumbles inside. I take advantage of the moment and dive between his legs. I remember to keep my elbows in the air and roll to cushion the impact, just like how Coach Broomes instructed Jared during a diving practice session.

"Josephine, get back here! I'm going to count to three!" Daddy yells behind me. "One!"

I race down the stairs and dash into the living room. Mr. Pimples, my blue-and-yellow angelfish, seems to gasp at my intrusion. He hides in the shipwreck in his tank.

"Two!" I can almost feel Daddy's hot breath on my neck. I dive and roll behind the couch, missing his grasp by an inch.

"Three!" As serious as the situation is, I can't help but think this is like a dodgeball game. I imagine the commentators cheering for me: "That was close! He nearly caught her there! Josephine Cadogan . . . what a player!"

I fling my hands in the air in dramatic style and leap over the couch, curving my back like a ballerina, but I botch my landing and stumble against the TV stand.

The framed picture of Mum flies high into the air. It's our favorite 'cause the photographer captured her with her head thrown back in mid-laugh, her curly black hair with blond highlights catching the sun.

The picture falls toward the floor, and both Daddy and I jump to catch it. I get a sharp flashback of "the incident" and come to a halt, leaving Daddy with the responsibility of catching Mum. His fingertips reach the frame, but it slides out of his grip. Thankfully, I am right there as backup to catch her in my cupped hands. I bring Mum toward my chest and hold her there with safe hands, just like I do with the cricket ball.

Why oh why didn't I do this at cricket tryouts last year?

Exhausted and panting, Daddy and I collapse onto the couch at the same time.

Daddy looks down at the picture of Mum, and then gazes at me. He does that sometimes—stares at me for no reason. I have Mum's flat nose and her messy, curly hair, but I have Daddy's dark brown skin, bushy eyebrows, and cynical glare. His eyes glaze over, and he retreats into that silent place in his head.

It's been almost five years since Mum's heart skipped

a beat and never found rhythm again. Still, I remember when Daddy stayed in that silent place for months, instead of a few moments, and Granny Margaret had to fly in from Guyana to take care of us.

Daddy takes Mum from my hands, and then, holding the frame as if it were a bubble about to burst, he puts Mum back in her rightful place. He shifts the frame toward the sunlight and uses his shirt cuff to rub a smudge off the glass.

I understand why women like my daddy. He is top-heavy, with broad, muscular shoulders developed from two decades of pulling tons of fish from nets. Since Mum died, he's gotten a few gray hairs at the sides of his head, but they don't make him look older, just wiser.

"Bean, yuh got to stop with this foolishness." He turns to me, scratching his chin. The beard is already growing back though he shaved two days ago.

He called me Bean, I think, relieved. *I'm out of trouble.*

I lift my chin in the air. "Daddy, she ain' right for you."

Daddy sucks his teeth. "You ain' even meet she properly, Bean."

"Daddy, if she can't deal with a little stink from fish guts, how she gine handle you when you come home from the sea? It is the same smell!"

Daddy opens his mouth and closes it. He contemplates, opens his mouth, and then closes it again.

"You!" He grabs for me, but this time it is playful. He digs into the spot below my ribs where I am most ticklish.

"Daddy, stop!" I squeal, but I don't really want him to. He kisses me on my forehead and I snuggle into his chest. There's only one thing that could make this moment better. I turn on the TV to the cricket match and then stare at Daddy's face.

My love for cricket began in front of the TV with my mum and daddy. I remember him squeezing me tight whenever a player hit the ball for six, and Mum raining kisses on my face whenever a bowler took a wicket.

I hold on to these memories because Daddy doesn't talk about Mum.

Ever.

It's like his love for cricket died with Mum. Now Daddy falls asleep whenever I ask him to watch a cricket game with me, and he always makes excuses when I ask him to help me practice bowling, so I'm forced to throw the cricket ball at plastic bottles instead.

Sometimes, I rest Mum's picture on the cushion next to me and try to recreate that atmosphere. It's not the same.

But I have a plan.

I've been working hard all summer doing chores for neighbors and selling sugar cakes and tamarind balls at the fish market. Daddy thinks I'm saving for a new cricket bat and ball, but I'm actually going to use the money to buy us tickets to the West Indies versus England match. The English cricket team only tours the Caribbean every two or so years, and even then, there's no guarantee that a game will be scheduled in Barbados. There's no way Daddy will be able to resist a chance to see our favorite team playing against our fiercest rivals.

I want Daddy to remember how happy cricket used to make him. And whenever he's not working, he'll want to spend all his free time watching and playing cricket with me. He'll have an extra-full, active life—no time for silly dating.

It's a win for both of us!

I struggle to contain my excitement as I picture me and Daddy at Kensington Oval, wearing our maroon West Indies shirts and doing the Mexican wave in the cricket stands.

Daddy gazes at the TV with an expression I don't quite understand. It's like hope and regret, combined with a little gas. He sniffs and rubs his nose with the back of his hand, untangles himself from my embrace, and gets off the couch. Then he pulls a pack of cigarettes from his pocket.

"Daddy . . ." I follow him until he slams the side door in my face.

He started the disgusting habit a few weeks after Mum died. I've been pestering him to quit ever since I saw a "smoking kills" ad where a man peels the skin off his face to pay for a box of cigarettes.

The cricket team's anthem, "Rally 'round the West Indies," starts to play in the stadium, and when the TV crowd chants David Rudder's lyrics, their unified voices soothe my troubled mind. That song almost brings me back to those happy days on the couch with Mum and Daddy.

Almost . . .

I look at the brown wig on the floor and squash the growing twinge of guilt. Women have always liked my daddy but he'd never paid them any attention . . . until this year. I need to revive his passion for cricket so he doesn't feel the need to meet any more "friends."

Daddy's cell phone rings on the counter, and I have to squint to see the words "Phyllis Landlady" on the small phone screen. Daddy's a simple man; he has an old cell phone with no internet and an old TV with one lone station.

Daddy comes inside and answers the phone. I wrinkle my nose in disgust at the strong cigarette smell.

"Yes, Phyllis," he says, then winces and moves the phone away from his ear. He glares at me.

Uh-oh.

Our landlady has already heard about the broken window. That's how fast news travels in Fairy Vale.

Everything else is slow, slow, slooowwwww. The hours seem twice as long, and every day feels like Sunday. Apart from the occasional church or community event or weekend karaoke at a rum shop, there's little to do. It's an ordinary, boring fishing village in Barbados.

"Yes, Phyllis," Daddy repeats, his voice flat and monotonous. "I will replace the 'ole window."

I try to sneak upstairs to my room while Daddy's still on the phone, but it's too late.

Daddy puts his phone on the counter. "'Old it right there, young lady. You're going to pay fuh this window."

I wheel around to see if the cigarette smoke has clouded his brains. "I don't have a job. How can I pay for a whole window?"

Daddy rolls his eyes at my confused expression. "Your savings, Josephine," he says in an irritated tone.

Not my money for the West Indies versus England

tickets! I inhale so sharply that all the saliva evaporates from my mouth.

I slowly release my breath, my mind racing with possible solutions. "Okay, Daddy, no TV for the rest of the summer vacation, okay?" I rush to turn off the television to show I am serious.

Daddy's sigh is loud in the empty silence. "Josephine . . ." It's never a good sign when he uses my real name.

"No TV for a month!" I offer, pleading with my hands. "And I'll clean the bathroom *and* do laundry every week!" Daddy knows how much I hate hanging clothes on the clothesline, but that's a small sacrifice to make to buy the tickets.

I wait for Daddy to accept my offer but he reaches for the broom and starts to sweep the glass on the floor.

"Sorry, Josephine, but we 'ave to use all your savings to pay for—"

I dash upstairs to my room before he can finish, hoping that his terrible thought will disappear with my absence.

This time, Daddy doesn't chase after me.

CHAPTER 3

I wake up even earlier than six in the morning to make Daddy's favorite breakfast—saltfish and bake.

This meal always puts him in a good mood, so it'll be easier to change his mind about using my savings to pay for the window.

Daddy taught me how to make both Bajan and Guyanese bakes. Guyanese bakes are different from Bajan bakes; the fried dough has no sugar and is much larger—almost the size of a grapefruit. I think Mum and Daddy used to argue about which bake was better, but I can't be sure.

I have to add that to the list of questions for Mum when I see her in heaven.

I glance at the brown masking tape over the hole in the window, and then focus on stirring the frizzled salt-fish just before it starts to stick to the pan.

That's how Daddy likes it. It reminds him of his home in Berbice, Guyana, before he moved to Barbados. He grew up in a fishing community like this one, where nets and colorful fishing boats line the seashore, and market people ply their trade, screaming, "Marlin! Tuna! Nine dollars ah pound!"

Before we came to Fairy Vale, we lived in a gated community near the city center. I don't remember much about the neighborhood, but I do recall a few things: playing in rosebushes, a bee stinging me on my nose, Mum humming in the kitchen, though I can't remember her voice. I have fragments of memories of Mum—her finger rubbing my cheek, breath that smelled like cinnamon, a tight hug—it's like a puzzle that only fits together in my heart, but I will never forget how happy I was when I watched cricket with her and Daddy.

I scoop some saltfish onto a plate and place the meal on the table when Daddy comes down the stairs. He frowns at me, but I know he's struggling to stay mad with the spicy aroma of fish mixed with onions, peppers, tomatoes, garlic, and lots of hot pepper in the air.

I give him my biggest, most innocent smile.

"The stove—"

"Turn off properly, yes."

He sniffs the plate. "You remember to add—"

"Yes." A pinch of cinnamon. It was Mum's special touch.

"And—"

"I'll feed Mr. Pimples after you let me start the car."

Daddy dangles his car keys in the air. I snatch them from his hand and hurry outside to warm up Jalopy. I swing the key in the ignition; it sounds like a nail scratching on galvanized steel, but soon the engine sputters on. In ten minutes, Jalopy will be ready to go.

When I shake the fish food into the tank, Mr. Pimples swims out from the shipwreck. He's named after the yellow spots on his face, and back when I got him I decided not to get any more fish in case they laughed at his acne. We've had him for three years now, which, according to Ahkai, is the equivalent of one hundred and ten fish years. I watch Mr. Pimples gobble a few of his flakes, and then join Daddy at the table for my own breakfast.

I wait until he finishes his last bite, leans back in the chair, and lets out his satisfied "Ahhhh." *That's my cue!*

"Daddy, about my savings, I—"

"No, Josephine, you 'ave to take responsibility."

"But pleasssssee, Daddy! I have plans for that money! Accidents happen all the time!"

"Bean, you're almost eleven now." My birthday is in forty-eight days. Every morning, I cross a day off the calendar in my bedroom with a red marker.

"Yuh big enough to understand things ain' as easy . . . fish scarcely biting, rent to pay, school uniforms to get . . ."

I jump out of my chair. "It's not fair! We can't have cable! I can't get a cell phone or a computer! Now I can't even buy tic—" I bite my tongue to stop myself from ruining my surprise.

"Young lady! Go and get your savings right now."

I stomp upstairs to get my piggy bank; it's a Coca-Cola bottle with a makeshift slit in the bottle cap. Then I drag my feet down the stairs, trying not to think about how many jingling coins and folded bills are in the bottle. I'm so upset I think I'm going to cry, but as usual, the tears don't come. There's little chance that I could save enough money again to buy tickets before they're all sold out, and it could be years before the two teams play again at Kensington Oval. My dream of getting the old cricket-loving Daddy back will soon become as distant as my memories of Mum.

"Please, Daddy," I whisper, my voice cracking.

Daddy rubs his temples. He does that when he's stressed out. "It's just me, Bean. I trying."

"That ain' my fault! It's not my fault!" I collapse on the bottom of the stairs.

Daddy pulls himself up from the table and shakes out his bad knee. Then, just when I think he's going to relent as usual, he pries the bottle out of my hand.

My heart drops to my toes.

Daddy bends down and holds my face in his hands. They are rough, but they still comfort me. "Let's pray today is a good day, okay?"

That gives me hope. Maybe if Daddy gets a big catch, he'll return my savings.

As if on cue, together we chant the Fisherman's Prayer:

> *God grant me the strength*
> *to reel in a big catch,*
> *courage to throw back what I cannot sell,*
> *and wisdom to know when to haggle.*

"Don't forget to—"

"Make sure all the windows are shut."

"And—"

"Lock the door."

BANG! Jalopy moves off. Most of the other fishermen are gone for days at a time, sailing as far as Tobago to fish, but Daddy is home every night. As always, I wave at Daddy until he disappears around the corner. Then, I search through the bushes until I find my cricket ball.

I head over to Ahkai's house, tossing the cricket ball into the air then catching it again. On Sunday mornings, most people are either sleeping or washing clothes, and the neighborhood is quiet. But it is never quiet at Ahkai's house. As soon as I enter the gate, I hear his mother yelling at his many cousins.

Though it's just her and Ahkai, the house is always filled with people. A stranger may think that Miss Mo is mean, but under the yelling she is super nice ... but *really* superstitious.

The door is never locked; instead there is a row of banana peels along a piece of wood on the veranda. Miss Mo says no thief would rob a house with banana peels on the outside, because they know that it's guarded by a baccoo, a tiny leprechaun-type creature trapped in a bottle. Once it's fed a constant supply of milk and bananas, a baccoo protects the house's owner when released. Most of the time I nod and keep quiet whenever

Miss Mo speaks about her strange beliefs, but Ahkai always tries to argue with logic.

"Mother, if a baccoo has enough strength to protect us from criminals, why is it not strong enough to break itself out of a glass bottle?" Ahkai will say, his face bent with irritation.

"The Lord does work in mysterious ways," Miss Mo will reply, and then start screeching a hymn, its crescendo drowning out Ahkai's arguments.

Nothing could change Miss Mo's mind, especially after someone *did* try to break into the house but slipped on a banana peel and broke a leg.

"I is a protected woman!" Miss Mo shouted after the thief as he limped away with the policeman. "De Lord and de baccoo watch over me!"

"Mornin', Miss Mo!" I say, still juggling the ball in my hands. She never acknowledges my greeting but gets annoyed if I don't give it. I won't forget the tongue-lashing I got when I once came into her house "without speaking."

Miss Mo is talking on the phone, washing dishes, and stopping one of Ahkai's younger cousins from stealing a hot dog from the frying pan, all at the same time.

Without thinking, I put the key that has fallen to the

ground back into the keyhole, so evil spirits won't be able to enter the house through the space. It's hard to keep up with all of Miss Mo's weird traditions, but I try. After all, Ahkai and I have strange habits too, and she doesn't question us . . . most of the time.

"Yuh want food?" shouts Miss Mo, moving the phone from her ear. Before I can respond, she slams a large plate of scrambled eggs and hot dogs on the table for me. It's easier and faster to just eat—I've learned not to argue. I lean over and start shoveling the meal into my mouth.

"Jo, sit down! If you stan' up and eat, de food does go down in yuh foot!" She attacks a pot on the stove with a bottle of Maggi all-purpose seasoning.

Miss Mo's shaped like an upside-down traffic cone, heavy on top, with large breasts, but with zero hips and slim legs. I guess she always sits while eating, maybe even to chew gum.

I pull out a chair and sit at the large mahogany table that swallows most of the kitchen.

"Drink some tea and break the air!" says Miss Mo, banging a large mug of hot chocolate next to my plate. "Next on the agenda, Marva," she says into the phone.

Miss Mo makes a living by renting out fish stalls at the

market, so she has plenty of time to be a board member on every committee.

"Look, you could believe the cricket association ask the Fairy Vale cricket team to escort the West Indies players onto the field, uh-huh, in that big match against England—"

I choke on my eggs.

"Jo! Tek yuh time and swallow!" Miss Mo yells. I nod and take a sip from the mug.

"Right, Marva, them invite we boys, and want the school to pay for extra tickets. I had to set them straight. FREE tickets for the cricketers' parents!"

I can't believe it. Those could be free tickets for me and Daddy! *And* I'd get to hold hands and walk onto the field with my favorite players. But I'm banned from trying out for the team . . .

It had taken me two years to build the courage to go to Coach Broomes's cricket tryouts. He'd taken one look at me sitting on the field and said, "Girls aren't supposed to play with boys." I still remember the surprise on his face when I stood up, and he realized I was tall enough to have a clear view of the bald spot in the middle of his head.

He reluctantly gave me a chance and put me in a

position near the edge of the field to test my agility. He assigned star-player Jared a few feet away from me.

I didn't have to wait long for a chance to prove myself. The ball got hit into the air and headed in my direction.

"Mine!" I shouted, laying claim to my catch. It was going past my head, but I knew I could get to it with one of those dramatic dives I'd seen in countless matches.

"Mine, mine," Jared said, looking up and coming in from the boundary.

"No, it's mine!" I was determined. I moved backward as fast as I could, still focused on the falling ball, and leapt in the air.

And then Jared collided into me.

That's my story and I'm sticking to it.

When I came to, Jared was moaning beside me, and Coach Broomes was leaning over him, ranting about why girls should never play with boys. And worst of all, when I got home, Daddy took one look at a tiny, *tiny* slash on my cheek and decided cricket was on the same danger level as skydiving without a parachute. He agreed with Coach Broomes that it was best I find another hobby.

I push the plate aside and hurry out through the

side door where I know Ahkai will be sitting on two blocks of concrete with a sharp knife, whittling a piece of wood.

I imagine most mums wouldn't approve of this dangerous hobby, but Miss Mo knows Ahkai can take care of himself. Plus, he comes first in our class every year, so she can't complain.

Ahkai holds up his latest masterpiece—a small mouse with its tail in the air. As soon as he stops carving, he rocks back and forth on the cement block.

"Cool! Is it for Simba?" I ask. Simba, his ginger tabby, jumps out from behind me to get his ears scratched. When he's satisfied, he strolls away and settles into his position—curled against Ahkai's hip.

Ahkai nods. "I am training Simba to become a hunter. This *Mus musculus* will act as the prey." I don't need a dictionary with Ahkai around; he knows the scientific name of every plant and animal.

Simba has already fallen asleep on his back with his legs sprawled out. He's more likely to cuddle with mice instead of killing them.

Ahkai goes back to cutting, and I look at the pendant around his neck—his lucky charm, a hummingbird in mid-flight. A symbol of our first encounter.

On my first day in Fairy Vale, a rainbow-colored hummingbird had flown right into the screen door and dropped to the ground. Of course, I freaked out, thinking the bird was dead. Then, Ahkai appeared out of nowhere like my guardian angel. He gathered the bird in his hands and stroked its head. Soon, the wings started to move, and then flap. The bird opened its eyes and flew out of Ahkai's hands into the sky.

Miss Mo crossed the street and looked on with surprise at the normally shy and reserved Ahkai whispering and giggling in my ear. She volunteered to keep me anytime Daddy had to work and stood with us while we stared at the sky even though the bird was long gone.

I move to the back of the yard, where I've lined plastic bottles along the edge of the outdoor sink.

Focus. Precision. Speed.

I bowl and the ball hits the plastic bottle right off the ledge.

Crack.

Yes! That'll show Coach Broomes.

My glee immediately turns to gloom. Every September, on the first day of the school term, Coach Broomes has the cricket tryouts for any "fresh blood." If only I could find a way to get on the cricket team . . .

I collect the ball and whistle a throw at another plastic bottle.

Crack. It flies off the ledge!

Bowled 'im! The crowd goes wild!

If I could just get Coach Broomes to see my bowling skills, I know I'd be one of the players walking onto the field at Kensington Oval, wearing the Fairy Vale Academy cricket team uniform and waving at my happy, re-energized daddy cheering from the stands.

Then, an idea pops into my head. Smiling, I sit on a concrete block and watch as the clouds crawl across the sky. My idea starts to formulate into a wild plan. All I need is a tight belt, a bit of luck, and a dash of faith.

I mutter a new Cricketer's Prayer under my breath:

> *God grant me the ability*
> *to accept umpire decisions I cannot change,*
> *courage to bowl a good spell,*
> *and the power to hold on to any catch.*

Ahkai clears his throat behind me. I turn around to see him holding out the cricket ball. *Oh, right . . .*

Crack. Crack. Crack. I quickly bowl the last three bottles from the ledge. Ahkai lets out a *"whoop whoop"* sound, celebrating the fifth crack, and then returns to his whittling station. He can concentrate now that all is right in his world.

I survey the scattered plastic bottles with pride. I can feel it in my bones.

I, Josephine, the cricket queen, will be crowned tomorrow on the first day of school.

CHAPTER 4

"Bean, get up! We late!" Daddy is shaking me. I'm not ready to move—I was counting wickets.

Daddy yanks the sheets off. "Is time fuh school!"

I groan and cover my head with the pillow, but he drags me off the bed. We argue with each other while rushing to get ready.

"Daddy, you taking too long in the shower!"

"Josephine, get back in there! You couldn't ah bathe so fast!"

"I want bacon and eggs, not watery sago porridge!"

"Look! Just eat a banana!"

"I can't find my other school shoe!"

"Yuh brain like a sieve! Now, where I put my car keys?"

"Yuh see, I get my sieve brain from YOU!"

And in the confusion, neither of us remembers to warm up Jalopy. I sit in the front seat, arms crossed and mouth pushed up to my nose, annoyed and flustered. Ahkai is in the back seat, playing with his hummingbird pendant, acting all oblivious to the tension. Daddy twists the key in the ignition, over and over again, but Jalopy only squeals in protest.

Daddy slaps the dashboard. "Come on! Come on!"

Jalopy gives in and splutters on.

"Yes! We will not be late!" Daddy does a little shimmy with his shoulders, and I can't stop a small smile from escaping.

Then—

BLAM!

The engine dies and black smoke gusts out from under the hood.

"We're going to be late," I announce, peeling the skin off the banana.

There's one blue-and-yellow Transport Board bus that passes through Fairy Vale, and it comes every hour if you're lucky, but it's always packed to the brim with people pressed together like melting marshmallows. Otherwise, it's about a thirty-minute walk to school—actually, forty minutes, since we have to keep turning around to carry Simba back home.

Daddy is quiet and I don't break the silence. He will need to find money to fix Jalopy. There's no chance I'll get back my savings now. *My plan to get on the cricket team needs to work . . .* I grip my backpack a little tighter.

We pass the karaoke rum shop, and though it's eight in the morning, four old men are hunched over, playing dominoes on a piece of board balanced on a rusty steel drum. They all wave at my daddy as we walk by. They'll still be there when we pass back again this evening.

Here's the truth about Fairy Vale. Everyone has a routine, and they're happy to do the same thing every day until they die. For them, there is nothing scarier than change.

Just when my feet are starting to burn, I see Fairy Vale Academy of Excellence in the distance, at the bottom of Coconut Hill. Guess how the hill got its name? Yup, because of the tall coconut palm trees along the border of the road. The coconut trees grow in two rows up the hill, as if they are lining up to receive blessings from the humongous silk cotton tree at the very top.

I've always wondered why the hill wasn't named Silk Cotton Hill. Those coconut trees are like mushrooms when compared to that monstrous tree, with their palms turned toward its muscular branches in worship. The silk cotton branches throw shade far and wide above the school, like the towering tree is reaching out to embrace the building . . . *or strangle it.*

Ahkai and I joke that the silk cotton tree pushed Fairy Vale Academy of Excellence off the edge, and it crash-landed into what is now the village's lone primary school. Don't mind its fancy name; at first glance, you'd think the building was an abandoned warehouse, with its yellowed, peeling walls in desperate need of fresh paint.

As we get near the school gate, we see Casper—my school's unofficial groundskeeper—lingering by the entrance and cleaning his fingernails with his favorite twig. Casper acts like he's guarding the prime minister. Under his watch, there's never a candy wrapper on the ground.

Casper was a successful broadcaster before his mind cracked. Early one morning, people found him roaming the streets in a torn suit, claiming that the Heartman kidnapped his wife.

I've heard stories about the cloaked figure who patrols the streets at night in a hearse-like vehicle, looking for victims. One time I came home late from Ahkai's house and Daddy rambled on and on about why children should never be alone outside after dark, and how the Heartman can rip the heart from your chest and offer the organ to the devil. Afterward we were both too scared to sleep and spent the rest of the night watching cartoons.

Casper claimed that the Heartman had no hearse but was instead riding a steel donkey—a cursed animal with eyes like fire. Legend says a person knows the steel donkey is coming for them when they hear the sound of chains dragging in the still of the night.

Last year I found an old chain, hid behind the tamarind tree, and rattled it when Casper walked by. No one saw him on the school premises for at least a month.

On seeing us approach, Casper ambles toward us, his four large dreadlocks swaying around his bony frame.

"Good morning, Casper," Daddy says in a flat voice.

Casper gasps and holds the twig—no wider than a pencil—in front of his face. When he whispers, the few dead leaves on the twig rustle under his breath. "Whew! He nearly saw me—that was close!"

I forgot to mention Casper got his nickname because he believes that, like a ghost, he has the ability to become invisible. He also acts like he's a narrator on the National Geographic channel.

Casper follows us. "These beasts can be very territorial, especially around their young. One false move, and I could have been a goner."

Daddy is now walking so fast that Ahkai and I struggle to keep up, but Casper, not letting the increased pace deter him, jogs next to us.

"This burst of speed is futile. Little do they know what awaits them in the closed canopy. Stay tuned."

It's a shame he won't be able to find out anything because he's not allowed in the closed canopy, also known as our classroom. Daddy accompanies us to class so he can apologize to our teacher. Mr. Atkins used to be a soldier, and he's super strict! He makes us stand outside the classroom if we're even a minute late from lunch.

But Mr. Atkins is not there. Instead, a small woman with rich brown skin and bleached dreadlocks sits at his desk, scribbling in an attendance book, while students are clustered together in little groups, chatting and showing off their new school bags, school shoes, and pencil cases.

The woman looks up and gives us a big smile. Bright red lipstick stains her teeth. Ahkai pretends not to see her, but when he walks by her desk, he does this little action—a combination of a bow and a nod. He sits in a corner, next to two boys comparing their new heights against a wall, takes out a heavy book, and starts to read.

Meanwhile, Daddy is wiping his hands on his shirt and trying to shake out a few of the wrinkles.

"Oh, wow, you're the tallest student I've ever had!" the woman says. At first, I think she's talking to me, but then I realize she's staring at my daddy.

"Oh, me? N-No, I'm just dropping off my daughter." Daddy doesn't get sarcasm.

"I'm Miss Alleyne, but you can call me Aurora," she replies, laughing at Daddy's awkwardness. I notice there's an extra emphasis on "Miss."

I narrow my eyes to slits. Her dress is bright with yellow sunflowers, and too tight to be appropriate for school if you ask me.

"I—I—I Mr. Cadogan," Daddy stutters. "Vincent." Miss Alleyne comes over to us and shakes Daddy's hand, taking far too long to break the hold.

"Oh, and how is Mrs. Cadogan this morning?"

"She's fine . . . wait, no! I mean, uh Bean's, I mean, my uh . . ."

I step between them and scowl at Miss Alleyne. "She's dead."

Daddy grimaces. Miss Alleyne finally pays me, the person she's supposed to be interested in, some attention.

We might as well get this over with. I have to go through this process with every new teacher. My mother can't ever sign a permission slip or collect me from school. You can't send a note to my mother about my bad behavior, and you won't ever see her at a PTA meeting. I'll never want to sing a song or make a card for Mother's Day. And, yes, this is awkward, but for you, not me.

"Oh, I'm so sorry," she says, reaching out to me.

"Where's Mr. Atkins?" I demand, dodging her touch.

"Mr. Atkins unfortunately had to travel, so I'm substituting for him this term. I just transferred from Ealing Primary in town."

Daddy scratches his nose. "Oh, well, if yuh need somebody to show you around—"

"We know a good taximan who can give you a tour!" I interrupt. Daddy gives a sheepish wave goodbye as I pull him out of the classroom.

He looks down at me, shaking his head. "You know, Bean, things will 'ave to change eventually," he says in a soft voice.

He's right.

I need to restore his passion for cricket to distract him from these women. He needs to fill those empty weekends watching cricket matches on TV with me, and he can use any free hours during the week to help me practice my bowling. I can't wait for all the fun we'll have together! He won't have any time or desire to give romantic Fairy Vale tours.

Cricket is much safer than heartbreak.

"Have a good day at work. Love you!" I close the classroom door.

It's hard to pay attention to the math lesson, despite Miss Alleyne's best attempt to make the useless subject interesting. What cruel person decided to put a large clock above the blackboard so kids could watch the tiny hands move so slowly they seem to be going backward? With every passing minute, I get more anxious about cricket tryouts, and more annoyed by the theory of mixed and improper fractions.

Briinnnggggg!

Lunchtime!

I fly out of my seat so hard the chair falls over. Miss Alleyne narrows her eyes and squeezes her lips together, but phew, she's still trying to be nice. I won't be fooled though. Nice teachers don't teach fractions on the first day of school.

Finally, Operation Cricket Queen can begin!

CHAPTER 5

The bathroom is packed so I sneak into the moldy toolshed at the back of the school. The area is out of bounds because of a small, murky swamp that fills up during rainy season, but students mainly stay away because of the fly-sized mosquitoes thirsty for blood.

I change into Ahkai's games outfit—dark blue track pants held up with a belt, and a large white T-shirt with Fairy Vale's elegant school crest. I push my curls into Daddy's old fishing hat, making sure to cover as much of my face as possible with its brim.

Ahkai is waiting for me under the tamarind tree. He took a break from reading in the library to give me moral support. I know my disguise has worked when I'm almost in front of him and he still has his standard blank expression. It's only when I smile that his eyes turn bright, and the dimple appears on his right cheek.

"Your transformation is astounding!" Ahkai tries to lift the hat.

I duck away and join the boys warming up on the field. The official members of the Fairy Vale cricket team are on the field as well, but they're sitting on the grass, sizing up the newbies.

They're mostly batsmen, able to hit the ball high into the air or far down the cricket field to get the winning runs.

But the team is missing good bowlers, someone to hurl the ball into the stumps, scattering the three wooden sticks like bowling pins to get the batsmen out.

Someone like me.

Coach Broomes blows his whistle and gestures for our group to come closer. He is a short man with a long gut that bulges over the top of his pants and almost reaches his knees. But don't be fooled by his physical appearance—I've seen him do one hundred push-ups with the rest of the cricket team without breaking a sweat.

"All right, this is what we gine do. Bowlers down there, batsmen over there." He points at the opposite ends of the pitch. The strip of ground is littered with footprints and skid marks from the batsmen running between them to score runs.

A boy puts his hand in the air.

"If yuh don't know which one yuh is, then get off my field. Yuh wasting my time," Coach Broomes says without looking up from his clipboard. The boy shrugs and walks off the field.

One down. Nine more to go.

We're to bowl to the batsmen, so Coach Broomes can analyze our technique and choose the best player. I'm so eager to fire the ball at them that I rush to be first in line.

Coach Broomes pushes the stumps into the ground with a worried expression, but he always looks that way, as if he's stuck in a cycle of bad news. I can't wait to bowl the ball into those stumps and send the three sticks flying into the air.

There's only one spot available on the team, and I'm going to make sure it's mine.

Jared walks to the crease with a cocky swagger. He's one of the few boys at school who is taller than me. My heart is pounding. He's the only eleven-year-old in the school with a slight mustache and hairy legs. He's super strong too—able to send a ball flying over the tamarind tree with a flick of the wrist.

This is just my bad luck; I'll have to bowl out the best batsman to guarantee a spot on the team.

Just like on TV, I see his player statistics coming up next to his face.

Jared Scott
Age: 11
Left-handed batsman
Strike rate: 108.92
Highest score: 212
Next victim: Josephine Cadogan

"First bowler!" Coach yells, but with a smirk on his face as he scribbles on his clipboard. I bet if he had his way, he'd hire a towel boy to wipe the sweat from Jared's face and feed him bottled water through a straw. And not just any kind of bottled water either—I'm talking about the expensive kind with bubbles.

I wipe my sweaty hands on Ahkai's pants, trying to decide what kind of delivery to bowl. I need to get Jared out by either forcing him to hit the ball into the air and taking the catch, or by hitting the stumps.

Focus. Precision. Speed.

CRACK!

Jared hits the ball into the air toward me. I jump to my

left, reaching for the ball to catch it. It slams onto my fingertips, but I can't hold on. My elbows slide into the ground.

"Ohhhhh!" A low moan from everyone on the field. *I nearly had him!*

"Good ball," says Coach Broomes, scratching his chin. "But your run-up is too short. Go back another four steps."

The cricket team is dead silent, shocked by the rare compliment from Coach Broomes. There is a "*whoop whoop*" cry in the distance. That's Ahkai cheering, and though I'm annoyed he could blow my cover, I do feel a little less nervous.

My sneakers pound into the ground as I run toward the pitch. *Hit the stumps. Hit the stumps.*

This time, the ball misses Jared's wild swing and hits the top of his leg pad. It's not exactly what I wanted but the ball would have knocked into the stumps. *He's as good as out.*

"HOWZAT!" I yell, appealing to Coach Broomes. I'm jumping up and down, already celebrating, but Coach Broomes doesn't raise his finger. Actually, he looks angrier than I've ever seen him.

Oh no . . .

I was so excited that I screamed "Howzat" in my normal, high-pitched girly voice.

So close . . .

I pull the hat from my head. My curls stay upright for a few seconds, and then flop down around my face.

"Josephine Cadogan . . ." He's so angry that his fingertips turn pink as he clenches the clipboard. "Suppose you did break your finger now? This ain' netball! This is a serious sport."

He looks around, as if checking to see if anyone is recording him.

"Please, Coach Broomes, just give me a chance," I beg. He knows I'm good. I see it in his face.

But Coach Broomes blows the whistle and walks away from me. He throws the ball to a boy with a tall flattop haircut, who races to the pitch to bowl.

I look at Jared, expecting him to be gloating, but I'm surprised to see pity in his eyes.

I don't know which is worse.

Jared glances over at Coach Broomes, and then focuses on the new bowler. Everyone continues to play the game like I never existed, like I'm another old ball with no thread.

The image of Daddy waving at me from the cricket

stands fades away, like a wave pulling a footprint from wet sand. I stand there on the field, crushing Daddy's hat between my fingers, wishing I could rip it apart and use the pieces to tie Coach Broomes to the tamarind tree until he's agreed to give me a fair shot.

I need to think. I need to scream. I need to be alone.

At first, I drag my feet back toward the school, but then I start to run, faster and faster. Everyone and everything is a blur. A confused Ahkai calling out to me. Children lining up with trays for school meals. The sleeping guard in the hut. The bees buzzing around brown coconut husks lining the road.

When my eyes focus again, I find myself on top of Coconut Hill, in front of the view of the shimmering blue sea—inviting, magical, but dangerous. I sit under the silk cotton tree, or as Ahkai would call it, the *Ceiba pentandra*, and stare at the ocean. My chest heaves and I sniffle, mucus running out my nose. There's no one around to hear my sobs, but I am crying without tears.

I think about the flattop boy walking out to the cheering crowd with the rest of the cricket team. I think about my mum missing another one of my birthdays. I squeeze my eyes closed as hard as I can, but as much as I try, tears refuse to fall.

The wind blows and some of the silk cotton fibers from the pods float down around me. The tree sheds once a year, and when the fibers drift onto school premises, the students with allergies start wheezing. Some parents, tired of their children reacting to the fibers, asked at a PTA meeting that the silk cotton tree be cut down, but Miss Mo wasn't having it.

"Duppies live inside that tree!" she yelled, her spittle flying on everyone at least three rows in front of her. "Them gine unleash them evil on everybody in Fairy Vale if wunna cut it down!"

Eventually, the government stated that the tree was of national importance, and so the school board was forbidden to remove it. But that "duppy in the tree" rumor spread throughout the school, so no student would even risk carving their initials into its trunk.

My frustration explodes in my chest.

I'm tired of rules!

I'm tired of people telling me what I can and cannot do.

Using a sharp rock, I press into the trunk of the silk cotton tree and scratch the letter "J" into the tough bark. I might as well be cutting with a Q-tip; the mark is almost invisible. I go over the letter again and again, and then—*Ow!* A splinter punctures my flesh.

A drop of blood appears on my middle finger and falls onto the bark, disappearing into one of the dark cracks. The wind gasps as it flutters through the branches, leaving a slight chill in the air that, for a moment, disrupts the scorching afternoon heat.

I take a piece of tissue from my pocket and press it against the graze. It stings! I can't even vandalize a silly tree without getting hurt. It's like I'm trapped in a maze, and there's failure at the end of each path.

"I hate my life!" I scream to the birds.

Out of nowhere, a strong gust of wind pulls the tissue from my hand.

I drop onto the ground under the tree and watch as the tissue flutters in the breeze and dances out toward the ocean.

CHAPTER 6

The light from the full moon shines through my window. I glance at the brass clock with bloodshot eyes.

Three in the morning. Too early for school.

It was easier to ignore the heaviness in my heart when I was focused on lessons and doing homework with Ahkai. But now that I'm alone, without any distractions, my failure to get on the cricket team haunts me, whispering dark taunts whenever I try to sleep.

Coach Broomes would have let you on the team if you were faster.

You're not as good a bowler as you think.

You're not good enough.

Now I'll never see Daddy's excitement when I hand

him those tickets. I'll never get to see the look of pride on his face as he watches me from the stands.

A cry cuts through the darkness. "No! No! I'm begging yuh!"

That's Daddy!

I jump out of bed and rush toward his bedroom. We never got around to closing doors. When I was younger, shadows came alive in the dark, so Daddy would leave all the bedroom doors half-open and keep the light on in the hallway.

Daddy's fighting with his bedsheet like a fish caught in a net. It's strange, but his hands are flailing around while the rest of his body is stiff, like he's bound by some invisible rope. He's covered in sweat, so much sweat that the entire bed is soaked.

"Daddy?" I pat him on his chest. His eyelids flutter but he doesn't wake up.

Years ago I was trapped in a terrible dream. When I closed my eyes, I was in the middle of the ocean about to be attacked by hungry sharks. When I opened my eyes, ghouls with slimy skin closed in over me. When I tried to get over to Daddy's room, there was a graveyard in the hallway, with bony arms pushing out of the mounds. I lay there in bed, opening and closing my eyes, screaming with no voice.

Miss Mo told me I had a spiritual attack.

"The next time it happen, repeat the Lord's Prayer, you hear me?" she said, after scolding Daddy for not having a Bible in the house. Then she flung holy water that she had borrowed from church in all directions. Ahkai did his best to disappear into the darkest corner of my bedroom, his face shining with embarrassment.

I pat Daddy's chest with a little more force. Strange . . . Daddy's usually a light sleeper—I can't even sneeze without interrupting his sleep. "Wake up!"

"No!" Daddy launches forward, almost slamming into my forehead. He looks around like a trapped wild animal, and clutches his head, his fingernails digging into his temples.

I am terrified. "Daddy, you having a nightmare!" I climb onto the wet bed and wrap my arms around him. He smells different . . . not of the aloe vera soap he scrubs with, or the sharp smell of dead fish after he comes home from the sea. It's like a combination of salt, seaweed, and musty socks. It's not unpleasant, but for some reason, it makes me uncomfortable.

Soon, Daddy's breathing goes back to normal, then he starts to chuckle.

"I supposed to be the parent, not you."

"We can switch every now and again, Daddy," I reply.

I'm lying. I don't ever want to see my daddy scared like this again. I don't want anything to hurt him ever again.

Daddy lifts me off the bed and I wince. I'd forgotten about the cuts on my elbows. I can't even call them cuts. Only the dark outer skin is missing. They're like white dashes with a few dots of blood.

"What 'appen?" Daddy asks, noticing my reaction.

"Nothing," I reply quickly, pulling my nightgown sleeves over my elbows. Daddy would be so upset if he knew I'd hurt myself trying out for cricket again. The scrapes are more painful than I expect but it's no biggie. I'll rub ointment on them later.

Daddy yanks away the sheets and struggles to pull a suitcase from under the bed. It's full of clean sheets and towels. His closet is still filled with Mum's clothes, so there's not much room for anything else.

"What were you dreaming about?" I ask, curious. *Was it zombies? Vampires? Spinach?!*

"I—I—I really don't remember," he says, taking the drenched pillowcase off the pillow. "I know I was cold"—he pauses—"and I was crying out but I didn't 'ave a voice. I remember fangs . . ." His voice trails away.

Dracula strikes again. Or maybe the soucouyant?

If a witch and a vampire were to have a baby, I imagine it would grow up to become a soucouyant. After the soucouyant sheds her skin and turns into a ball of fire, she slips through keyholes and under doorways and sucks on the blood of children. I had to sleep with Daddy for a week after Miss Mo told me why she keeps the key in the lock. I don't understand why none of Miss Mo's folklore creatures are nice and generous. Why are they always out to kill or torture humans?

The moonlight reflects across an object on top of the bedside table.

A strange comb.

Daddy sees me staring and holds it in the air. It's beautiful—looks like brass, with coil markings carved into the handle. Tiny sparkling jewels are scattered throughout the markings and seem to change color every time I blink. It looks hundreds of years old, like it belongs in an ancient Egyptian museum.

"Catch it in my net last night. Was 'oping Miss Mo would gimme a good price for it, but she just vent some foolishness about a River Mumma. Like Barbados got any real rivers."

Daddy rolls his eyes. He's always boasting that all the small Caribbean islands could fit in the Essequibo River in Guyana.

"River Mumma?"

"A mermaid who combs her 'air on a rock by the river.

She does supposedly put spells on fishermen and cause them to crash their boats."

"I'm glad we don't have any real rivers, then," I reply, laughing.

"In Guyana, we call them fairmaids, and they 'ave long golden hair. Same superstitious nonsense on every island, but everybody know it ain' real. Sometimes I worry 'bout Maureen, 'ear?"

That's Miss Mo for you. When collecting fish from the boats, she throws a silver dollar in the water and walks backward out of the sea. She says it stops evil spirits from following her.

After Mum passed, Daddy would take me out fishing with him. He taught me how to put fuel in the motor of *Joanne*, his small red-and-yellow fishing boat, renamed after Mum, and sometimes, he would even let me steer. Whenever I went out on *Joanne* I felt at peace, and she rocked me to sleep many times.

One day at the beach, me and Ahkai were chasing sandpipers when the birds fluttered out to sea, then landed on top of a jagged rock shaped like a raised fist.

Ahkai started to cry and pointed to the rock.

"Oh no, baby, nobody can go out there," warned Miss Mo. "Them rocks haunted, yuh know, full of duppies!"

Ahkai stopped crying and gave her a blank stare. He was cynical, even back then.

"Give and it shall be given unto you," she prayed, before hurling a silver dollar into the sea.

I darted into the water in an attempt to catch the coin. There was shouting all around me, but I ignored it, thrusting my hands forward and kicking, enjoying the feeling of the water parting through my fingers. I don't remember a time I wasn't able to swim; I felt at home in the sea.

I dove underwater to look for the dollar, and then was yanked backward out to sea. The ocean had turned into a large pot, and the wave was a cou-cou stick, stirring me like I was okra in cornmeal. The first gulp of salt water burned my throat and nose. I tried to scream for Daddy, and I remember nothing more after that. I regained consciousness on the shore, choking and spluttering and swearing never to go into the sea again.

Poor Ahkai, who never learned how to swim, was catatonic after watching my near-death experience, and refused to go near the shoreline.

Daddy always complains that he's the only fisherman with a child who is afraid of the ocean.

Now Daddy examines the comb, poking one of the jewels. "Probably cubic zirconia."

I reach for the comb, but Daddy jerks it away from me. "Go back to bed, young lady. You 'ave school in a few hours."

"But I'm not sleepyyy!" I whine.

"Well, I might as well do your 'air, then." Daddy pulls at one of my tight curls.

I yawn, patting my mouth. "Boy, I'm so tired, Daddy. Night night!"

Daddy blocks me from launching off his bed. Every Sunday, Miss Mo used to trap me between her slim-but-powerful legs and yank at my hair until I was sure my scalp would come off with the braid. One day, after a painful yank, I temporarily lost my mind and bit down into her thigh. Miss Mo refused to plait my hair again, so Daddy had to learn.

At first, he was awkward, and I had to go to school with jagged parts, and cornrows that unraveled after a few hours. But now he's very good at it, and much gentler than Miss Mo. Still, I brace myself, 'cause my hair hasn't been combed since last week. It will be like combing a knitted shirt.

But the pain never comes. The comb glides through my curls, as easy as warm butter on a biscuit.

This is weird.

Again and again, Daddy moves the comb through my

hair. I'm worried the brass will scratch my scalp, but it's like a massage.

Daddy rests against my back and hums a new tune. It's definitely not one of the mellow reggae songs he plays on Sunday mornings. I can feel the tension in his abs as he tries to maintain a falsetto note, almost as high as a whistle from the kettle.

"Hey, Daddy, can I get blond highlights? You know, like Mu—" Daddy stops humming and jerks the comb from my hair. The soothing atmosphere is now tense. I lose my nerve to say the "M" word.

"Like a movie star?" I finish the sentence. Daddy exhales and doesn't answer me. Instead, he continues to run the comb through my hair, this time without the humming. I relax against his chest and close my eyes.

It's like I am on *Joanne*, rocking back and forth on the waves, listening to chirping crickets and gazing at stars.

For the first time in my life, I fall asleep while getting my hair done.

CHAPTER 7

Miss Alleyne gushes about percentages like she's recapping the latest episode of her favorite TV show.

I try not to slam my head into my desk. My brain is so overwhelmed. I have to remember schoolwork from last year, understand the numerous topics we've covered in the last two days, and figure out how to raise money for the cricket tickets before they're all sold out.

I'm in class four now, the final year of primary school, and only eight months away from taking the distressing Common Entrance 11-Plus Exam that everyone is so nervous about. Even Daddy, who seldom asks me if I have homework, insists I have to "buckle down and work hard this year."

As if Ahkai will allow me to slack off. He wouldn't let us have any fun this summer until I completed all the math and English exercises he designed for me.

Ahkai will most likely get the highest marks on the exam and pass to the top secondary school on the island. Meanwhile the highest I've ever come is thirteenth, but I have to get into the top secondary school next year with Ahkai. I can't imagine going to another school without him . . .

The thought is scary enough to make me sit up in my seat and focus on Miss Alleyne, who's now pointing at the problems on the whiteboard.

"So you can apply this basic strategy to calculate VAT, or even sales tax!" She pauses and beams at us like she's expecting applause.

Ugh. I'd so rather be playing cricket right now . . .

Ahkai shoots me a disapproving look.

It's like he can read my mind!

Briinnnggggg!

That's lunch.

This time I stay in my seat, not sure where to go. Normally I'd rush off to the cricket field and eat lunch in my hiding spot behind the tamarind tree while waiting for the cricketers to arrive. Today I can't bear to watch them practice drills, knowing I've lost all chance of getting on the team.

I don't want to go to the library with Ahkai either; he spends most of lunchtime with his head buried in a book. In the end I decide to stay in the classroom and pretend to study percentages. I glare at the numbers so hard they start to look like ants moving across the page.

"Josephine, can we have a word?" Miss Alleyne comes over and sits in the seat beside me. Ugh, now I may have to do schoolwork for real. I angle my body away from her, thinking of an excuse to leave.

"When I was eleven, my teacher asked all of the class what we wanted to be when we grew up. When my turn came, I got to my feet, like this—" Miss Alleyne shoots out of the chair. I notice she's wearing flat green ballerina shoes, and not fancy heels like most of the other female teachers.

"I want to join the military, sir!" Miss Alleyne salutes the whiteboard.

I'm really not accustomed to teachers talking about their personal lives. Mr. Atkins has been our teacher for three years and I don't even know his first name.

"Um, that's cool, ma'am," I mutter. I bite the inside of my cheek and inch closer to the door.

Miss Alleyne sits back down in the chair. "No it wasn't

cool at all, at least not for the teacher. He laughed and told me that girls don't belong in the Defence Force."

I swing around in my chair so fast I almost fall off. I feel a burst of rage for eleven-year-old Miss Alleyne, and almost-eleven-year-old me.

But Miss Alleyne smiles and places a white envelope on my desk.

"I saw what happened on the field yesterday and had a word with Coach Broomes. He wasn't on board at first, but later he agreed to put you on the team on a trial basis."

My hands tremble as I reach for the envelope. Coach Broomes isn't one to change his mind, so I'm afraid to unfold the paper in case it turns out to be a math assignment in some sadistic prank. Is this really happening? I have another chance? I don't believe it until I read the permission slip. All I need is Daddy's signature to make my cricket dream come true.

"Now, it's only for the friendly match coming up," Miss Alleyne warns, "for you to prove you can"—she pauses, then rolls her eyes and does air quotes—"keep up with the boys."

The dark cloud above my head vanishes in my joy. I'll be so far ahead of the boys I'll look like a speck of dust to them. I'm going to bowl so fast the ball will leave a trail of smoke behind it. They'll chant my name in the stands.

Imagine how well I'll play when I get to wear my own gear, and I can be myself! I know I can impress Coach Broomes and be made a permanent member of the team.

I open my mouth to thank her, but no words come out.

"I know," Miss Alleyne says with a wink, then leaves me alone in the classroom. I sit there, staring at the letter and daydreaming about Daddy singing in the stands at Kensington Oval.

It usually takes forever to get home from school with Miss Mo. She always pulls the car off the road to chat with someone. Most of the time it's much faster for me and Ahkai to walk home; sometimes we even hide in the bushes if we see her little Toyota Starlet in the distance.

I'm fidgeting with anticipation, unable to keep still in the back seat. Ahkai looks up from his book and asks a question with his eyes, but I want to give Daddy the good news first. I can't wait to see his face when I tell him I made the team *and* that I'm going to get passes to the West Indies versus England match!

His life is going to become so full once he remembers

how much he loves cricket. No time for dating at all, and that's good for both of us; all he needs is me and cricket.

We turn onto our street and I get a glimpse of Daddy by the kitchen window. He's home early! I'm so excited I jump out of the car before Miss Mo brings it to a complete stop.

"Sorry!" I yell, before she gets a chance to scold me.

I push open the door and swing my backpack against my chest, pulling out the permission slip. That's when I notice the pair of crystal heels on the WELCOME mat.

My racing heart crashes to a dead stop and a knot tightens in my belly.

It's been less than a week since his last "friend" left in a tizzy without her hair. I wasn't expecting another woman for about three months!

How did she slip past the first line of defense? Daddy never goes on a date without consulting me first. I am not prepared, and I am unimpressed with this breach of protocol. I push the envelope back into my bag.

Daddy appears from the kitchen and gives a little start when he sees me. "Oh, Bean, I ain' 'ear you come in!" It's normal for his fishing clothes to be old and stained, but his shirt has a long rip from the neck to the middle of his chest. He must have really struggled to restrain the fish today.

"Look what I catch!" He gestures behind him.

Though the boards in the kitchen are creaky, I do not hear her coming. She wears a white-and-red cotton dress, which floats like a cloud around her curvy body. As she approaches, her hips move from side to side, as if her bones are made out of springs.

Her gigantic, thick afro brings her almost to Daddy's height. She's slicked down her hair at the side, giving it a wet, yet not greasy look. Her smile is so big I can't see the color of her eyes. She wears a small silver hoop in her nose, and her teeth sparkle like they've been polished. Her cheekbones are so pronounced it looks like she's sucking in her cheeks, and this should be unattractive, but those cheekbones combined with a long neck bring an air of elegance. She seems too glossy, too refined; if she stood still long enough, she could be mistaken for a poised mannequin.

"I hope you like fish." If a harp could speak, it would sound like her. She presents a large tray of flying fish with flair, like she is a model on a game show. I'm sure my face has the same expression as those dead fish—mouth wide open in paralyzed horror.

"Bean, this is Mariss. My lucky charm!" Daddy lifts me up and swings me in the air. "The boat was full with fish today!" Even in my dismay, I take note of the fact that Daddy referred to *Joanne* as "the boat."

He kisses me hard on the cheek, then turns to Mariss. "I'm going to cook my famous fish soup for you tomorrow!" he says, taking the tray from her hands.

"Cook for *me*?" Mariss's eyes widen just enough for me to notice they're dark brown. Daddy puts an arm around her shoulders, and they return to the kitchen.

This isn't a good time for company. She can come back in about ten years.

I follow them, wheels already turning in my head, and sit on a stool by the bar to watch them bone the fish. Daddy is explaining to Mariss that after the scales, head, tail, and fins are removed, you slice on either side of the backbone.

Daddy pulls the backbone out with the knife, and Mariss grimaces.

"This is Bean's favorite," he says, pointing to the fish melts stuck on the sides of the backbone. When I first found out the melts were the flying fish's eggs, I tried to spit them back out, but the fried delicacy was so delicious I couldn't stop chewing them.

Mariss pokes the fish guts with a long manicured nail and wrinkles her nose with disgust. She rubs her hands against the counter, like she's trying to wipe away germs.

Daddy laughs. "Mariss sells jewelry in the market, so she's accustomed to gems, not guts," he tells me, adding some onions to the chives, garlic, cloves, and green herbs in the food processor. He's going full gourmet, even making the Bajan green seasoning from scratch as a marinade for the fish.

Daddy pushes a button on the food processor and Mariss jumps back like she's been shot with a bazooka, putting her hands over her ears. Daddy's so focused on pouring vinegar in the chute that he doesn't notice Mariss gaping at the appliance like it's an angry howler monkey. Nope, this woman is too weird. I'd be doing Daddy a favor getting rid of her.

I look at the bucket next to Mariss, once again filled with fish scales, bones, and guts. It worked once before, didn't it?

"I wanna help!" I jump from the stool and speed over to them before Daddy can stop me. Then, I pretend to stumble.

To my surprise, it is Mariss, not Daddy, who reacts first and attempts to catch me. I still manage to knock the bucket from the counter and the contents spill all over the right side of Mariss's light cotton dress.

"Josephine!" Daddy snarls. I try as best as I can to look remorseful. "Mariss, I'm so sorry!" He grabs a kitchen towel from the sink and starts wiping the slimy muck from her arm.

Mariss stares down at her dress. I wait for her to march out in disgust, but to my astonishment, when she looks up there is a smile on her face.

She turns to my daddy and pushes out her right leg. The water has made the light cotton material almost transparent. Mariss slowly lifts a shapely leg out from the dress. There isn't a blemish on her ginger brown skin, as if a mosquito or sand fly has never touched her.

Uh-oh. Who knew it was possible to look seductive while covered in fish guts?

Mariss pats the top of my head. "Don't worry, Josie Sweets, your daddy and I forgive you, right, Vincey?"

Josie Sweets?! *Vincey?!*

Daddy gulps and nods, mesmerized by Mariss.

I have to put an end to this right now. "Sorry that you have to go home to change, Mariss," I say, already heading to the door.

"Oh, I'm sure your daddy has a shirt or something I can wear," she replies. She lifts her leg even higher and pulls a fish bone from the material.

Daddy snaps out of the trance. "I—I—I, yeah yeah,

uh . . . upstairs, uh, bedroom. Josephine, clean up this mess!"

Daddy disappears around the corner to go upstairs, and Mariss moves to follow him.

Over my dead body. Daddy's about to be too busy with cricket to care about dating. I'm not going to let this woman ruin my plans at the last minute.

I lean against the fridge and stick my foot out to the wall, creating a human barrier gate in the kitchen.

Mariss raises an eyebrow. It's so strange. A raised eyebrow usually causes a wrinkle around the eye, or even in the forehead, but Mariss's face is smooth like new Plasticine.

"Sorry, no entry." I dare her to challenge me.

But Mariss smiles and leans against the kitchen counter, moving her hand up and down along the wall, as if she is a handyman checking for cracks.

"You don't like me, nuh?" she says, running her tongue across her bottom lip.

"No," I reply, deciding to get straight to the point. "Leave my daddy alone."

Mariss makes a "tsk" noise. "I sense your father is a special man, Josie Sweets. I don't blame you for being overprotective, but you can trust me. I won't hurt him." She bites on her top lip. Is she thirsty or something?

"Don't you have lip balm?" I ask. It's a little disturbing to speak to someone who is licking their mouth every second.

"Oh, I have a gift for you!" Mariss opens a black case on the counter. I can't help but be intrigued. It's my natural response to the word "gift."

She takes out a necklace made of transparent and silver beads that reflect a blue undertone, with a small, brass spiral pendant. I move my barrier foot to get closer to it. Light catches on the beads, making them sparkle like stars.

"You'll have to take really good care of it." Mariss steps toward me, the necklace hanging from her middle finger. "Like I'll take care of your father."

I pull my eyes away from the necklace. "You think you can bribe me with a piece of cheap jewelry?"

Mariss doesn't seem bothered by my insult. If anything, she smiles even bigger. "Not a bribe. A gift," she says, gently resting the necklace back in the case. "But I'll keep it safe till you change your mind."

"I never change anything!" I respond, frustrated by her calm, confident demeanor.

Mariss bends down until we're at the same height. Her deep brown eyes shimmer like they're filled with an ocean of tears. The sound of the sea crashes through my brain, like someone has put a conch shell by my ears. I can almost feel the waves caressing my insides, flowing through my body and washing all my fears away. I am so light, so light that I could float up into the sky and swim in the clouds. Suddenly, I feel choked up, like I want . . . to cry.

I blink, then squeeze my eyes shut until the feeling has passed. What is happening? When I open my eyes, Mariss is so close that if I flared my nostrils, the tips of our noses would touch. I take a step back.

Mariss straightens her shoulders and smirks at me. "You will."

"Look 'ere." Neither of us heard Daddy coming down the stairs. He holds out a light blue material with a floral pattern. I've never seen this shirt—wait—what?

Mum.

That's one of Mum's dresses.

"Oh, isn't this lovely!" Mariss sashays over to Daddy and drapes the dress over her arm.

I cannot fathom someone else's skin touching Mum's clothes. I am numb, trying to process the information, trying to understand Daddy's betrayal.

"It belong to my . . . my . . ." Daddy swallows and looks at the ground. "My late wife."

What is happening?! It's like I'm in a horror movie,

right at that moment when the monster reveals itself and is baring its pointed teeth at its prey.

"Well, she had wonderful taste," says Mariss. But she's not looking at the dress; she's looking at my daddy . . . and my daddy's eyes are fixed on her.

"I'll make sure to wash it and bring it back for you."

"No, you keep it," Dad replies to Mariss with a sad smile.

"I'll give you some money for—"

"Absolutely not!" Daddy exclaims, cutting her off. "You don't 'ave to give me anything. It's a gift."

"A gift for me?" Mariss says in a confused, soft voice, as if no one in the world has ever thought to give her a present before. They both inch closer to each other. It's like they've forgotten I'm in the room.

I drag the stool across the kitchen boards and the screechy noise jolts them back to reality. Mariss winces and covers her ears.

My backpack rocks on the stool and falls to the ground. The cricket permission slip flies out of the bag.

"What's this?" Daddy asks, picking it up.

"Um, we can talk about it later. It's"—I glance at Mariss—"personal."

"Oh, let me get you some privacy," Mariss says, and hurries to the door.

Finally.

Mariss closes the side door—with herself inside! All I can do is stare and blink as she locks the door and struts back over to me and Daddy.

"Bean, I ain' sure," Daddy says as he reads the letter. "Remember you 'urt yourself last time."

A pang of worry shoots through me; it never occurred to me that Daddy wouldn't sign the paper.

"Daddy, I'll be careful, I promise!" I cry. I hold on to his arm and look at him with wide eyes. "You should have seen me at cricket tryouts. I was the best bowler there!"

He sighs and runs his hand down my cornrows. Got 'im! I can already see Daddy waving from the cricket stands.

"Cricket!" Mariss exclaims, then makes her "tsk" noise again. "I was wondering how you got these."

Mariss lifts my elbows with soft hands, revealing the scrapes underneath. I rubbed the ointment on them this morning but they look much worse than they feel, with the skin an angry purple and pus forming around the edges.

"Cheese on bread!" Daddy holds his head, then runs his hands down his face. The scrapes might as well be stab wounds.

I try to pull away from Mariss's touch, but then I feel

the weirdest sensation. Like if lightning and ice water were flowing through my blood at the same time. Hot then cold. Cold then hot. Then, a sense of satisfaction, like I've just finished eating a tasty meal.

Mariss lets go of my elbows. I shake my head, trying to regain focus.

I stare at her and tilt my head to the side. But she interprets my look as an invitation to give her opinion.

"All sports are dangerous," Mariss chimes in. "There aren't many games where someone doesn't get hurt." She looks into the distance, and then a light bulb seems to go off in her head. "How about joining a choir? Do you like to sing?"

Daddy folds the permission slip and puts it into the kitchen drawer—the same drawer he puts random things he has no use for, but doesn't want to throw away.

"Bean, you soon off to secondary school. I sure it will 'ave a girls' cricket team. Best you wait till then."

I sag against the counter. Right now, Daddy and I were supposed to be celebrating and making cricket plans together. It all turned out so wrong, but I just can't give up, I can't.

"But, Daddy—"

"Where's your bathroom?" Mariss interrupts me. "I want to change into this gorgeous dress."

She holds on to his arm, and Daddy guides her up the stairs like she's just had knee-replacement surgery. Mariss looks over her shoulder and winks at me.

I'm so angry I could burst into flames.

Ding! The match has begun.

This means war.

CHAPTER 8

"Come in, Alpha Mike. What's the status? Over."

Ahkai answers right away.

"This is Alpha Mike. Alpha Mike. Alpha Mike. Alpha Mike. Alpha Mike. The item will be secured in T-minus five minutes, ten seconds after the parental unit exits the lavatory. Over."

I peek through my bedroom window for any sign of Mariss. Daddy said she would be here by six when he sat me down to deliver the "be on your best behavior" lecture.

The weather is bizarre today. At this time of year, the sun would be under the horizon, but right now, it's burning hot and bright, and large raindrops beat down on the roof. They say—and when I say "they" I mean Miss

Mo—that this means the devil and his wife are fighting over the cou-cou stick.

The doorbell rings.

Right on time. I rush downstairs to greet her.

Operation Sticky Buns is my greatest masterpiece. I'm 150 percent confident it will get rid of Mariss, once and for all. Daddy may be a little disappointed, but it's best to get her out of his life so he can focus on cricket.

Even though it's warm outside, she's wearing a long-sleeved white-and-red pantsuit, looking like a piece of Christmas candy cane. There's a brass spiral pendant hanging from her neck. It's almost identical to the one she tried to give me, but these spirals are thicker.

"Sisi!" Daddy exclaims, and hugs her.

Great, now she has a pet name too.

I swallow my irritation and beam at her. "Hi, Mariss! Hope you are well!" Daddy looks at me with suspicion.

"Hello, Josie Sweets!" She leans over to kiss me, and I get a whiff of her perfume. I can't figure out the smell, but it reminds me of sea spray and sand.

"Want some guava-pineapple juice?" I ask, turning to go into the kitchen.

"That sounds amazing!" exclaims Mariss, as if she's never tasted juice before.

"Oh no, I'll get it!" Daddy guides me to the dining table and forces me to sit. "Do not move from this chair," he whispers into my ear.

He turns to Mariss. "We also 'ave passion fruit juice and lemonade. Which one you want?"

Mariss gives him a mischievous smile. "You."

I suck my teeth in disgust, especially after Daddy grins like a schoolboy with a new marble. He brings me a cup of juice and gives me the "yuh better behave yourself" look, then heads into the kitchen with Mariss.

There is a quick sequence of five knocks on the back door, and Ahkai marches inside like a soldier. He stares straight ahead, not looking at me, but flashes a small plastic bottle in my direction.

Everything is going to plan . . .

For all the years I've been over at Miss Mo's, I've seen them run out of milk, sugar, eggs, even toilet paper, but there are always Epsom salts in that house. Miss Mo believes the white crystals can cure everything from cold, flu, headache, giant African snail infestations, spiritual attacks, acne, to everything! But if you eat them, well, all I'll say is that one of Ahkai's younger cousins once shoved a handful of the crystals into his mouth and a few minutes later, we heard terrible noises coming from the bathroom.

I eye the guava-pineapple juice in Mariss's hand and smile. There is a tube of superglue in my jeans pocket. As soon as Ahkai gives the cue, I'll go and line the toilet seat with the sticky liquid. Mariss wants to be part of the family? I'll make sure she *sticks* around long enough for Daddy to hear those awful noises coming from her. She'll be too humiliated to look him in the face ever again.

I do my evil laugh under my breath.

Daddy brushes something away on Mariss's cheek. She holds his hand and kisses the back of it.

There's no time to lose.

Ahkai is still standing by the door, staring straight ahead. I give a sharp nod and he marches toward the kitchen.

"What gine on, son?" Daddy says to Ahkai, even though he never answers. "This is my, uh, friend, Mariss. Mariss, this is Ahkai. 'E's the strong, silent type." Daddy turns to stir the pot on the stove.

"Looka you. Aren't you a cutie!" Mariss goes over to Ahkai and puts her juice down on the bar near him. She gives him a big hug, crushing his face under her bosom.

I can't see Ahkai's expression, but his body loses the army stiffness, and his right hand starts to shake.

All he has to do is sprinkle the salts into the cup. No

one is looking! Ahkai's hand inches toward the glass. I am so nervous I start gulping down my juice. *Just a little farther!* Then Ahkai pauses, and he lifts his hand in the air. *This is the moment! This is it!*

Ahkai puts his hand around Mariss's back and nestles into her embrace.

I almost spit out my drink.

This can't be happening.

Mariss gives Ahkai one last squeeze, and then turns to Daddy. "I don't like this microwave thing at all, Vincey. I like to see the fire under my food."

"You and my mother would get along," Daddy replies with a chuckle.

Mariss pinches Daddy's chin. "I can't wait to meet her."

Ahkai, with his face shiny and eyes bright, at least has the decency to look ashamed. He walks over to the dining table with bent shoulders and sits next to me.

I am furious. "Gimme the package," I hiss.

Ahkai shakes his head.

I reach under the table and pry the bottle from his hands. It falls onto the ground and rolls under the TV stand.

I leap from the table.

"Miss Josephine..." Daddy warns from the kitchen. He's pouring water into a large jug of ice. Mariss is on her way with the big pot of daddy's famous fish soup, made with coconut milk, sweet potatoes, and dumplings. I smell the aroma of garlic, basil, and fresh rosemary.

"I forgot to feed Mr. Pimples." I get the fish food and take my time shaking the flakes into the tank. Mariss puts the hot broth on the table and scoops a portion out for Ahkai.

Daddy is staring at me so I can't reach for the bottle. Mr. Pimples swims to the top of the water, gulping down the food, surprised at the rare treat of being fed twice in one day.

Mariss puts out a serving of soup for Daddy. *That's my job!* She doesn't know he likes as many pieces of sweet potato that can fit into the bowl, and one single dumpling.

Maybe I make a noise because Mariss looks across at me, pursing her lips. She comes over to the tank and peers at Mr. Pimples.

"What an interesting-looking specimen," she says. Mr. Pimples stops eating and hides inside the miniature sunken ship. "Beautiful, but she's so lonely."

"Mr. Pimples is not a she!" I protest, but in truth I have no idea how to tell the difference between male and female angelfish. It never occurred to me that Mr. Pimples could actually be Miss Pimples.

"Poor thing is desperate for a mate," Mariss says, ignoring my outburst and tapping the glass.

"I am not getting another fish," I declare, making sure I enunciate every word. *Who does she think she is, coming into my house and trying to change things?* "Anyway, Mr. Pimples may get angry and eat the fish."

"Only if he gets in her way." Mariss smirks and looks at me, but this time I avoid her eyes.

Mariss takes the fish food from my hand and gives the bottle a long sniff. "Hmm, soya bean, yeast, wheat, brown rice . . . this is very healthy."

Is she a bloodhound?!

"But you shouldn't keep *Miss* Pimples so close to the speakers. The vibrations could kill her. Vincey, can you help move this?"

"I can do it," I say. The tank isn't that heavy.

"And open up those cuts?" Daddy snaps. "Leave it!"

I roll my eyes. I had forgotten all about the silly scrapes. I can barely feel them.

Wait a minute . . .

I run my hands over my elbows. The skin is smooth.

I take a quick peek, and all that's left of the bruises are two tiny black lines. This is so weird . . . I've never had cuts of any kind that healed so quickly before.

Daddy comes over to lift the tank, and I shove the

thought aside. He looks at me, and then over to my empty seat. I drop my head, return to the table, and slouch in my chair.

"Sit up, Josie," says Mariss. "We ladies have to mind our posture. Back straight, shoulders back."

I glare at Mariss and open my mouth to tell her some ladies need to mind their business, but I take one look at Daddy's face and sit upright in my chair. I glance over at Ahkai for moral support, but he's just watching Daddy and Mariss with this dopey smile.

My own best friend . . . a traitor.

Mariss gets Daddy to move the tank over to a mahogany table near the back door. That small change makes a big difference to me. Not even the delicious smell of Daddy's soup and homemade cassava bread could make me feel better.

I notice Daddy staring at Mariss with a dreamy smile too. He puts an arm around her shoulder and now they're close together, looking at the picture of Mum, but their backs are turned to me so I can't see any expressions.

If I don't think of a new plan soon, Mariss is going to win this war . . .

Then, I spy a second chance of defense. Daddy's homemade hot pepper sauce! Daddy says the local

Bajan pepper sauce doesn't make him sweat, so he invented his own. A pepper sauce made with blended Guyanese wiri wiri peppers and vinegar. Daddy wears bright yellow gloves and green goggles when he's blending the sauce, looking like some sort of tropical mad scientist. Even if I'm upstairs in my room, the pepper fumes make me cough like I'm in a burning building. Just three drops of Daddy's blend are enough to make him take off his shirt and stick the fan on his body.

Miss Mo calls it the devil's seasoning.

I remove the cover that controls the drops and dump almost half the toxic pepper sauce into the pot of soup. Ahkai twitches like he's been electrocuted.

I give him a smug smile. Miss Mo always says, "If yuh don't have horse, ride cow." I just had to find another solution. Operation Sticky Buns may have failed, but now we have Operation Fire Mouth.

Daddy and Mariss return to the table and sit opposite Ahkai and me. I scoop some of the soup into a bowl for Mariss. Daddy helps me guide the bowl over to her to make sure I don't spill the hot soup "by accident."

"Thank you, Josie!" she exclaims.

I have no choice. I am forced to put soup into a bowl for myself. I pile bread onto my plate.

Daddy reaches for the pepper sauce, and after glancing

at Mariss, shakes one drop into his bowl. I guess he is self-conscious in front of his new ladylove and doesn't want her to see how much he can sweat. He doesn't even realize that half the pepper sauce is missing.

"Pepper, Mariss?" I ask with an innocent smile. Ahkai's eyes widen, and he starts to rock in the chair.

"No, no, it too strong," says Daddy. "She can't 'andle that."

Mariss scoffs. "I can handle anything." She puts not one, but four drops of pepper sauce into her bowl. Daddy's eyes bulge open.

I couldn't have planned this any better. She won't look so attractive to Daddy when she's coughing up soup and drowning in her own runny nose. If I'm lucky, she'll hurl her guts onto the dinner table.

Mariss brings the soup to her nose and sniffs it. She pauses, and inhales long and deep.

For a moment, I'm worried she can smell the toxic pepper fumes, but then she puts a spoonful of the broth into her mouth.

I wait for the explosion.

She frowns. "This is . . ." I hold my breath in anticipation.

"Delicious!" she says, and puts another spoonful into her mouth. Mariss applauds Daddy's cooking skills with four slow, deliberate claps.

Daddy chuckles and begins to eat his soup. Ahkai gazes at Mariss, waiting for her to clap a fifth time. Growing impatient, he claps his hand once, completing the quintuple, and bites into a dumpling.

This isn't possible.

The pepper must have gone off.

I put half a spoonful of the soup into my mouth.

Then, I experience the full might of the devil's seasoning as if I'd died and shot straight down into the flames of hell.

My insides are burning and I cannot breathe! I cry out and start gulping water from the jug. It's making it worse! My mouth is melting!

"Bean, Bean?" Daddy cries out. "What 'appen?" I jump up and down, pointing at my mouth and the pepper bottle.

Daddy sucks his teeth. "Josephine! Stop being so dramatic!"

But I can't respond. I drop to the ground, wriggling like an earthworm. It feels like molten lava rolling down my throat, into my chest, annihilating all my internal organs. Snot runs from my nose. I'm pretty sure it's going to be followed by blood, then what's left of my brain.

"Enough!"

Daddy lifts me up and marches to my bedroom. He

throws me onto my bed. "Stay in 'ere until you stop behaving like an infant."

He slams the door, leaving me in the dark to ponder how it could all have gone so wrong. I hear someone opening the door, and I already know it is Ahkai.

"I'm sorry. I'm sorry. I'm sorry," he repeats. I don't let him finish. I throw a pillow behind me, not even turning to face him. Ahkai sighs and closes the door, leaving me in complete darkness.

Then Ahkai opens the door again, leaving a small crack. Warm light floods the bedroom, scaring the dark away.

I don't know when I fall asleep, but when I open my eyes, there is an oval moon in the sky.

My belly rumbles with hunger, but my throat is still raw. I doubt I can ever eat Daddy's soup again; the thought of it makes me nauseous, but I suppress the feeling, not wanting to relive the trauma through wiri wiri pepper vomit.

I get out of bed and stick out my tongue in the mirror. It's swollen to twice its normal size and cracked like an erupting volcano. The pale pink color is now a soft red, and it hurts when I move it up and down.

Mariss is not normal. No one can eat all that pepper and have no reaction. I can't wait to show Daddy my tongue so he can drop to his knees and beg my forgiveness.

I step into the hallway and pause when I hear a giggle coming from downstairs.

A fake, high-pitched, gargle-guzzling giggle.

Mariss's giggle.

With each step toward the sound, I feel like my heart is expanding, and expanding, until it will burst. From the bottom of the stairs, I stare at Daddy and Mariss cuddled up on the couch, her head resting on my place on his chest. Daddy kisses her on the forehead, and I turn away when she tilts her mouth up toward his.

If I could have avoided this moment by eating fresh wiri wiri peppers every day for breakfast till I was eighteen, I would have done it in a heartbeat.

CHAPTER 9

I didn't think it was possible, but I'm too angry to enjoy cricket.

The team is practicing their fielding skills—catching incoming tennis balls, then running between cones. I return the ball to Coach Broomes and speed to my next mark, but I can't help but fume at the incident from this morning.

I had woken up early to clean the kitchen as a surprise for Daddy. I scrubbed the stove, the oven, and even the fridge. It was sparkling! But all my hard work was overlooked when Mariss waltzed into the kitchen and had a sneezing fit. Apparently, she's allergic to the cleaning product.

And Daddy had the nerve to scold me! Told me I

should have checked with him. They've been dating for two weeks, and I already need permission to clean my own kitchen!

Swoosh. A tennis ball flies past my ear, and Coach Broomes rolls his eyes.

I have to focus; I can't let Mariss steal both my daddy *and* this chance away from me. In one hour, the Fairy Vale cricket team will be playing O'Brien Primary in a friendly game, and I'll get an opportunity to seal my place as the team's star attack bowler. Daddy will *have* to let me play once he hears how important I am to the team.

And then he'll forgive me for forging his signature on the permission slip too. I had snuck it out of the drawer and signed it this morning before we left for school. I swallow a rising bubble of guilt, thinking about the fraudulent document in Miss Alleyne's desk, but no one has higher stakes in this game than me. I have to work hard to impress Coach Broomes so I can change Daddy's mind before the actual cricket tournament begins next month.

Instead of warming up, Jared and some of the other cricket boys are lounging under the tamarind tree, treating cricket bats with linseed oil. They're all in white-and-blue Fairy Vale polos, specifically made for the cricket team, whereas I'm in a plain white T-shirt.

They all laugh, probably at another one of Jared's corny Ossie Moore jokes. Daddy and Jared would get along; he loves Ossie Moore jokes too. He can't get enough stories about the Bajan folklore character, legendary for his idiocy.

I grit my teeth and try to ignore the slackers under the tree.

I wonder if Mariss is allergic to linseed oil.

Ugh, I just can't get her out of my head. I hate to admit that since she came into Daddy's life, the catch is always plentiful. In the short time, he's cleared off the rent arrears, and Jalopy is all repaired and has a new dark green shade, though I do miss the rattling.

Even Daddy's gray hairs seem to be turning black again. He's happy, and I should be happy he's happy, but instead I am upset that he's so happy while I'm so unhappy.

Coach Broomes blows a whistle and we all gather around him. He silently counts the heads, his finger hesitating for a second when it passes over mine.

"All right, boys, uh, people. We want to start this season on the right foot so don't take this game for a joke." He flicks something off his tongue. "Now, as you know, some of the class fours went to a seminar today so we got exactly eleven boys—uh, people."

Ahkai was the first student to sign up for the seminar. He wanted to prepare for the transition to secondary school as much as possible.

"So nobody"—Coach Broomes pauses and looks right at me—"no-bo-dy get injured or cause any injuries."

I avoid his eyes. Now I know why Coach Broomes decided to put me on the team on a trial basis. Without eleven players, he would have had to forfeit the game. Today may be my only chance to prove myself.

"Come, let we sit and talk strategy." Coach Broomes turns a page on his clipboard and walks away. I follow him and the team until I realize they're on their way to the dressing rooms.

Please, no . . .

If they go inside, I won't be able to follow. Someone's going to realize that, right?

But Coach Broomes struts down the stairs and ducks into the dark dungeon that is the boys' changing room to discuss the game plan. The rest of the team chatters among themselves, not one person noticing that I am left behind. I kick the grass, and instead of lingering by the smelly door, I head to my safe space on Coconut Hill.

I sit and stare at the sea, hoping the sound of the waves will soothe me, but it's like my soul is outside my body, looking down at my pathetic, slouched figure, unable to feel the tiniest bit of joy. I wonder if, somewhere in the great, big ocean, there is a fish that gets upset every time the tide changes.

I run my hands along the coarse trunk of the silk cotton tree, looking for the letter "J" that I carved into it, but there's nothing there. My small act of defiance has left no lasting impact. All the effort I put into making that mark, all the pain, all for nothing. Even when I try, I can't get anything right. Maybe it's a sign I should just disappear—from school, from home, from life.

It's almost time for the match. I dust the dead leaves from my pants and head back to school. I'm approaching the gates when Jalopy's squeaky horn stops me in my tracks. The sound rattles my bones and I shove my hands into my pockets so Daddy can't see them shaking.

Of all the days for him to surprise me at school! My eyes dart around the area, checking to make sure there's no one around to blow my cover. I have to get rid of him before he finds out I'm playing cricket.

"Need a ride?" Daddy sticks his head out the window. He looks like a model in one of those advertisements, with his eyes full of laughter and mouth open after hearing that he's just saved a bundle on car insurance. He's holding hands with Mariss in the front seat, who's wearing a shirt with a mess of white ruffles at the neck, looking like a long-lost musketeer.

"Aurora! 'ow are you?"

Please please please let there be another person named Aurora nearby. I squint behind me, but there's Miss Alleyne, smiling at Daddy in a purple-and-blue flower print dress. I can hardly breathe; my lie is closing in, ready to drop and burst like an overripe mango.

Daddy gets out of Jalopy. Instead of letting go of his hand, Mariss scooches over to the driver's seat and gets out of *his* side of the Jeep. This is sadder than the lovesick couples in those soap operas I'm not supposed to be watching.

"Aurora, this is my, uh, friend, Mariss," says Daddy with a flush.

"A *very* good friend," Mariss says in a singsong voice.

Daddy and Mariss stare into each other's eyes and grin. I'd roll my eyes if I weren't so anxious. I need to get rid of Daddy before Miss Alleyne spills the beans.

"Are you here for Josephine's cricket match?" Miss Alleyne asks, fidgeting with her fingers. She seems uncomfortable with their gross affection.

Daddy breaks away from Mariss's spell. "What cricket match?"

Coach Broomes blows his whistle, long and hard. I wish I could turn into a handful of sand and let the wind blow me away from this situation. Miss Alleyne looks down at me, and after a moment, understanding dawns in her eyes. I stare at the ground to avoid her look of disappointment.

"Josephine Cadogan, I specifically tell you not to play cricket! You elbows already mash up, you tryin' tuh dead?" Daddy shouts.

"Don't be too hard on her, Vincey," says Mariss, in that sugary tone reserved for Daddy. "I did silly things when I was a little girl too."

I can feel everyone's gaze on me, waiting for my response, and I open my mouth to defend myself. I want to argue that tiny scratches on the elbows do not lead to death, that cricket is anything but a silly game, and also apologize to Daddy and Miss Alleyne for lying. All these thoughts merge together and tumble out as a long groan. I rub my temples, just like Daddy does when he's overwhelmed.

"Daddy, I just wanna play. Just this once, please." I speak in a careful, controlled manner, as if I'm now learning English, and then I slump against the school gate in frustration. "You know what? It doesn't matter. If

Coach Broomes has his way, I won't get to touch the ball anyway."

Daddy unravels his fingers from Mariss's clutch. Now it's his turn to rub temples.

"Your daddy and I don't want you to get hurt, Josie." Mariss arches her eyebrow at my slouch and I pop upright, squaring my shoulders. I forgot I must always be like a soldier about to salute.

Miss Alleyne clears her throat and she steps closer to Daddy. "Josephine was wrong to lie but she really is a good bowler. Come see for yourself."

I'm not sure how Mariss is doing it; she's still smiling, but the look she's giving Miss Alleyne is poisonous enough to wilt those purple-and-blue flowers on her dress. Daddy looks at Mariss, then back to Miss Alleyne, and I hold my breath, waiting; I can almost hear the wheels turning in his head.

"Listen," Daddy says, frowning at me. "I gine let you play this one time—"

I squeal, and fling my arms around his waist, my fear now replaced with determination. Now I have the chance to impress both Coach Broomes *and* Daddy.

Daddy ruffles my hair. "Just be very, very, very careful, Bean."

"I don't think this is a good idea," Mariss warns, but I'm not foolish enough to stick around while she changes Daddy's mind.

I tear through the gates with fresh energy, sprinting toward the pasture.

CHAPTER 10

All the Fairy Vale players are on the field, with two O'Brien Primary batsmen having a discussion in the middle of the pitch. Seems I've missed the coin toss, and O'Brien Primary has chosen to bat first. *Yes!* Now I'll have the chance to show off my bowling skills immediately.

Coach Broomes is on the edge of the field arguing with the umpire, which is all pretty commonplace, except for the look of relief on his face when he sees me approaching.

"Get on the field!" he yells, and I rush past him, heading to a vacant spot on the boundary. The umpire sucks his teeth but walks onto the field to start the match.

An O'Brien batsman soon hits the ball in my area, and

I grab it from the grass and, without losing a second, zip it back toward the stumps. I groan as it misses the right stump by an inch!

"Cadogan, next time throw the ball to the wicket-keeper!" Coach Broomes yells from the sidelines. Coach has so little faith in me, but my disappointment turns to delight when Jared yells, "Good throw!"

"Aha! Here we have lion cubs pawing willow wood, traversing the vast land for pleasure and exercise!" Casper appears behind Coach Broomes, hollering commentary. "I will try to get a closer shot!"

The game is delayed for a few minutes while parents and teachers chase him off the field.

The batsman hits the next ball in my area again, but instead of throwing the ball to the wicketkeeper, I take a chance and aim for the stumps again.

Crack! The O'Brien player stares at his broken stumps in disbelief.

Cheers erupt around me, and all of a sudden I'm engulfed in sweaty armpits—the smell of victory! Daddy beams at me from the stands and thrusts a fist in the air. His support makes a bigger impact than the hard slaps of approval on my back. I feel like I could float up to the clouds.

After breaking the opening partnership, the rest of the batsmen fall like dominoes. Though Coach Broomes doesn't give me a chance to bowl, he can't deny I've made a good contribution to the team.

But when it's Fairy Vale's turn to bat, a massacre unfolds. I watch openmouthed as most of the batsmen get out without scoring. Only Jared has a good game, knocking off most of the runs by himself. By the time it's my turn to bat, Fairy Vale needs one more run to win the game, and I am the last hope for the team.

It's so quiet, even the birds are watching.

Coach Broomes drops onto the bench, dejected. He doesn't even bother to give me advice; he's already given up.

I walk onto the pitch, trying to remember batting tips, and Jared meets me at the crease.

"Just play a defensive shot." His eyes have lost their mischievous sparkle; they're dark and determined.

Daddy looks like he's ready to leap over the railing and strap me in a bulletproof, or I should say ball-proof, vest. Mariss looks grim and whispers in his ear, but his worried expression does not change. I'll be surprised if I get his permission to play again.

The O'Brien players huddle, trying to decide what

delivery to bowl to me. My heart is beating so hard I can hear it in my ears. The Fairy Vale team is on their feet; Coach Broomes is quiet, clenching his clipboard.

The bowler runs toward me, his face and arms glistening with sweat. I focus on his hand and recognize that he's going to bowl a slower ball. It's a trick I've used many times, hoping the batsman will make a hasty swipe at the ball and get out. I can win this for the team! I can be the hero.

I bring my bat down in a perfectly timed play and welcome the surge of exhilaration. I'm ready for the moment the ball makes contact to score the winning run, for Coach Broomes and the rest of the team to rush toward me in celebration, for Daddy to remember there's no better feeling than when your cricket team wins a game.

Then the ball stops.

In. Mid. Air.

What?!

It's too late to stop my huge swing. The ball suddenly curves under the bat and hits into the stumps.

That crack shatters my heart into a million pieces. I wait for the umpire to signal a no ball and report the opposing team for some kind of ball tampering. *How does a ball stop in midair?* But the umpire raises a finger in the air and takes off his hat.

It's over . . . I missed the chance to make the winning run; I've let down the team, and myself. And Daddy.

The O'Brien Primary players and supporters cheer and rush onto the field. Jared groans and covers his face with his hands. Coach Broomes slams his clipboard into the ground and stomps away. I search for Daddy in the stands, desperate for a sympathetic gaze, but he's gone.

I twist my head about until I see Daddy and Mariss walking toward me. Daddy's head is bowed but Mariss is staring right at me, and then, her eyes flash yellow.

I rub my eyes and when I take another look, Mariss's eyes are normal, though her face has that smug expression.

It must have been the sunlight.

"The vile vixen. She's free."

I turn to see Casper backing away, his face frozen in terror. He gawks at Mariss, snaps his precious twig in two, and forms a cross.

"Our heaven, who art in father, hallowed be thy kingdom." Casper whirls around and sprints so fast toward Coconut Hill that he may have qualified for the Olympic track team.

Daddy holds out his arm and I hide my face in his side. He gives me two sympathetic taps on the shoulder. I can almost hear him say, "Dear dear, you tried your best."

All I can think about on the ride home is that ball stopping in midair. No one else seemed to notice, but I know I didn't imagine it. Maybe the O'Brien players hid some kind of robotic chip inside the ball and used a remote to control its movement. But I have no proof, and I definitely can't count on Coach Broomes to investigate. My blunder is the best excuse for him to deny me a place on his team. I press my face into my hands to stop myself from screaming. Whatever hope I have left of seeing the West Indies match with Daddy floats away, leaving a writhing ball of misery in its place.

I want to hide under my pillow until this day is over.

I step inside the house and notice two large black suitcases by the back door. Mariss unbuttons the top of her long-sleeved, frilly shirt. Her spiral pendant gleams against the lace. She moves toward one of the suitcases and unzips the top, searching through its contents.

No no no no.

Daddy clears his throat and steps next to Mariss. "Bean . . ."

No no no no.

Daddy's mouth is moving, but I can't hear a word. I turn to look at the picture of Mum on the TV stand; I need to see her laugh to calm my insides.

But her picture is gone.

CHAPTER 11

I stare at the calendar on my wall. Thirteen days since Mariss moved in—thirteen days that have felt like thirteen years. I can't stop thinking about all the strange things that have happened since she came into my life.

She's staying with us while her roof is being fixed but doesn't know how long that's going to take. She took Mum's photo to her jeweler to have the frame polished and still hasn't brought it back. All her meals look like the moss floating on top of a swamp; I even caught her trying out Mr. Pimples's fish food, which she claims is "packed with nutrients." She's full of static electricity and her eyes flash yellow like spotlights.

Casper saw it too. What is a "vile vixen"? I wish I could ask but no one's seen him since the cricket match.

I can't believe I want Casper's opinion, but who better to consult in this situation? A cricket ball stopped in midair, for goodness sake!

I sigh, but then chide myself for being gullible. Even if vile vixens, soucouyants, duppies, or any folklore creatures were real, they would never choose to live in boring ol' Fairy Vale.

I toss my ball into the air for the umpteenth time and watch as gravity brings it down into my waiting hand. It's official; this ball doesn't freeze in midair. I've avoided Coach Broomes since the friendly match. I don't want to give him the opportunity to officially tell me I didn't make the cut for the team.

Sand flies attack my legs, and I push aside my thoughts to get the insect spray. It's time to dispose of all unwanted pests, and I'll start with these bloodsuckers first, then figure out a way to get rid of Mariss so my life can return to normal.

"Daddy! Where's the spray?" I yell, scratching at the welts rising up on my skin. I barge into his bedroom. He sits on the bed, yawning, though it's only eight p.m.

I show him the red splotches on my skin. "You've been neglecting your fatherly duties! There's no spray, no repellent in the house, nothing!"

"Oh, Josie Sweets, don't blame Vincey," Mariss says,

looking in a mirror. She adjusts her red robe and pats her afro into a perfect circle. "I had to get rid of those chemicals! We gonna use some natural products."

I'm speechless. Mariss brushes her hand against the wall. *Why does she do this?* Always rubbing against walls, counters, my daddy . . .

"Lavender is a natural insect repellent, trust me." She gets a bottle from the dresser and rubs me down with sweet-smelling oil. At that moment, another sand fly bites me through the thick layer of lavender oil. I slap at my arm and pull away from her.

"I HATE this! These bugs need to die! *YOU* need to die!"

Mariss exhales a long breath, so hot it could melt the plastic smile that's still on her face. I am so surprised by its heat I forget my rage.

"Josephine! That's it." Daddy grabs the cricket ball from my hand. Wait, is he confiscating my cricket ball? He's threatened so many times, but he's never actually done it. And with my savings gone and me avoiding Coach Broomes and the cricket field, who knows when I will be able to replace it.

"I'm sorry, Josephine, but you 'ave to learn to be respectful," he says in a firm, deliberate voice, as if he's been rehearsing the speech. Then he leads me out of his bedroom, and guilt flashes across his face before he gently closes the door. The soft click snaps me out of my shock.

He's shut me out. We *never* lock doors in this house.

I bang on his door, shouting his name. With every second that Daddy ignores me, our special bond slips further and further away, and I feel his devotion to me, to our family, crumbling apart. It's like he's forgetting me, forgetting *us*, just like how he's forgotten Mum. My heart hardens so much it feels heavy, like a rock inside my chest.

Without thinking, I storm out of the house and down the street. It's only when the anger subsides that I realize I have no idea where I'm going.

The full moon brightens the sky.

I've never been outside this late and I try my best not to think about the Heartman, lurking in the darkness and waiting to shove me into his hearse.

All the noises I hear from my bedroom window when I'm gazing at the stars now seem a lot more threatening. The crickets' chirps seem frantic, as if they're all warning me to go back indoors. A bird squawks like it's being ripped in two. Even the howling wind sounds like ghouls moaning in misery. I become hyperaware of the fact that I am alone.

The leaves on the mango trees tremble in the wind.

Miss Mo has always warned me and Ahkai about douens—the spirits of children who died before they were baptized. They pass for normal children in the dark, but they have no face and their feet are turned backward.

"Never, and I mean never, follow a child who's calling your name! Especially if the sound coming from the bush!" she says with her bulging eyes open to their fullest. "Children that follow douens through the trees don't ever come back."

"Josie..."

I wheel around, my arms in a karate stance. I took one introductory class before losing interest.

The streets are well lit and the road descends into a sharp corner, so I should be able to see anyone in the distance. But there's no one around; even the park with four broken swings and rusty monkey bars is deserted. Nothing moves, except for a piece of caution tape fluttering in the wind by an open drain.

A shadow flickers behind the bars, and I see the shape of a big afro.

"Mariss?"

The shadow makes strange twitchy movements in the darkness, and it warps into something like a giant octopus with tangled tentacles.

I yelp and fall back into the road, scrambling to get away from the area. The bottoms of my sneakers slide against the gravel and the sound is as loud as a nail scratching against a chalkboard in the silence.

Then, bright headlights blind me. *I'm going to be roadkill . . .*

I cover my face and wait for the impact, but it never comes. Nothing happens. The driver doesn't say anything. There's just silence. My heartbeat quickens again. I risk a peek through my fingers and see a big black vehicle.

I hide my face again.

It's not a hearse . . . it's not a hearse . . . there's no such thing as the Heartman . . . there's no such—

"Young lady, what are you doing out this time of night?" says a deep, authoritative voice.

My heart jumps out of my chest. I roll out of the road and hit into the sidewalk. When I look up, I see fluorescent green-and-blue squares at the side of the Jeep.

It's not the Heartman . . . it's worse! It's the po-po! A policeman looks out the window of the Jeep, frowning at me. His large round face almost blocks out the full moon.

All the heat rushes out of my body, and I break into a cold sweat.

The one time I'm out "after dark" and I get caught. To

be honest, I don't even know if it's a crime. Suppose I have to spend the night in jail? Suppose they call my daddy and tell him to come bail me out? Omigod, I can't even imagine how much trouble I'll be in if he discovers I was out "after dark." I'd prefer to spend the years in jail and let Daddy think I'd been kidnapped.

I turn and pelt down the road toward my house.

This was a bad idea. Even as I run, I know it. I am close to home when the police Jeep pulls up next to me. I stop running and, with a hung head, walk the last couple of feet to my house with them driving beside me. I feverishly pray they will let me go inside without making a scene.

And that's when they blast the sirens. The lights immediately turn on at Miss Mo's.

Busted.

Two policemen step out of the Jeep in their gray-and-dark-blue uniform, their faces tense, like they're in the middle of a tough math exam.

Ahkai appears beside me with Simba in his hands, stroking his fur. Behind him is Miss Mo in a flower-print nightgown, with her hair in curlers and covered with a head tie.

"Wuh gine on?" asks Miss Mo. "Somebody dead?"

"Constable Cumberbatch here. This is my partner, Constable Jones."

Constable Jones breaks his silence with a voice much softer than I expect. "We found her loitering in the street, ma'am."

"I was not loitering! I just wanted a lil fresh air, that's all." I roll my eyes, hoping Miss Mo will see that everyone is overreacting, but Ahkai frowns at me.

Mariss seems to appear out of nowhere. "Josie Sweets!" She runs toward me, her arms outstretched, and gives me a big hug. I'm overwhelmed by a weird salty smell. "I was so worried! Thank you, officers!"

Miss Mo examines Mariss from top to bottom. "So you is Vincent new woman."

Mariss has on a light poncho dress, and her skin shines like it's lathered in baby oil. On inspecting her, Constable Cumberbatch's face transforms with a smile, from stern to almost juvenile.

"Young lady, you shouldn't worry your mother," scolds Constable Cumberbatch.

I plan to yell "It's no big deal!" but instead, "She's not my mother!" comes out of my mouth.

There is an awkward silence. Mariss stiffens, and her whole body gets hot again, like an iron that's just been plugged in. I pull away, checking to see if her skin has reddened, but she only has her cold, drawn smile.

Miss Mo purses her lips in disapproval. "Where Vincent is though?"

I look up at Daddy's window. It's still dark. *How come the sirens didn't wake him up?*

"Sleeping." Mariss moves forward to shake Miss Mo's hand. "Well, it was nice to meet you—Ow!"

Lovable, tender, gentle Simba has scratched her hand. Mariss jumps back, and Simba lets out a long hiss. I didn't expect Ahkai's hunter training to be so effective, and neither did he, since he's looking at Simba like the cat just yelled "hakuna matata."

I stroke Simba's fur with new appreciation, and he calms down but keeps his eyes focused on Mariss. It's my turn to look smug. Mariss nurses her hand and sneers at me and Simba.

"That gine leave a scar," Miss Mo warns. "Get lil Mercurochrome or—"

"I'll deal with it, thank you very much," Mariss says in a disturbingly quiet voice. "It's getting late and Josie has school in the morning. Good night."

She holds my hand in a firm grip and leads me inside. I tug my hand, but I can't pull away. Her grip is as tight as a Jaws of Life.

I look back and the officers are getting into their Jeep. Ahkai shrugs and follows Miss Mo back home. Simba, still in Ahkai's arms, turns his face toward my house, staring at me and Mariss like we're prey.

Mariss releases my hand from her death grip once we're inside and locks the door. I'm about to give her a piece of my mind when I notice the shipwreck in the fish tank is upside down and there is no sign of my fish.

"Wait, where's Mr. Pimples?"

"Oh no, it must have been that cat," says Mariss with fake concern. "Somebody must have left the door open."

I lift the shipwreck out of the tank and shake it, hoping Mr. Pimples will plop out and mouth, "Here I am!"

Nothing.

"Mr. Pimples . . ." I whisper. I dip my hand into the tank, running it through the tiny blue pebbles. Mucus blocks my nose, and I start to sniffle. I race upstairs to Daddy, desperate for him to comfort me.

When I burst into his room, Daddy's out cold, body straight like he's in a coffin, not the usual catspraddled position with one foot hanging off the bed.

"Daddy, Mr. Pimples is gone!" I shake his shoulders. "Daddy!"

But he doesn't wake up. I pummel him on the

shoulders so hard that my fists hurt, my cries of "Daddy" getting higher and more frantic. Mucus runs down my nose, and my eyes burn.

Why isn't he waking up?!

Is this how Daddy felt when he woke up and found Mum next to him, cold and silent? I put my ear to his chest and collapse against him in relief when I hear a faint heartbeat.

I race to the door, but Mariss blocks the doorway.

"Something wrong with Daddy!" I scream, trying to push her aside. But she grips my shoulder with an iron hand and gently cups my face with the other. The light in her eyes shifts like the moon behind a cloud.

"Let it go, Josie."

"Move, woman!" I struggle to get away, anxious to call for an ambulance.

"Josie, you have to learn to be respectful. I just want us to be a happy family," she says in a matter-of-fact, casual tone, as if my daddy isn't on death's door. "You have so much to be grateful for."

Then, Mariss whispers in a voice so soft I have to read her lips to hear the words. "Wake up, Vincey."

Daddy jumps up from the bed like a fire alarm went off in his ears. "Wh-What? Wuh 'appen?"

"Daddy!" I launch myself into his arms. He lifts me up

and carries me to my room. I turn my face away from Mariss as we pass by.

"It's okay, Bean," he says, kissing me on top of my head and lying down next to me. "You just 'ad a bad dream." He hums his weird falsetto tune while I lie on his chest, listening to his strong, steady heartbeat.

I can still feel Mariss's hot breath. The ghost of her tight grip lingers around my wrist. I see Mariss's silent whisper of "Wake up, Vincey" over and over again. There's no logical explanation for everything that happened tonight.

Mariss isn't just an annoying girlfriend; she's much more threatening than that. I struggle to make sense of my thoughts.

It's unbelievable, but I think Mariss may not be human.

CHAPTER 12

Everyone around me is clapping and laughing, but I am worried.

It's been twelve days since the "after dark incident" and I've been watching and waiting for something out of the ordinary to happen. It's like waiting or an explosion, except you're not sure if there's even a bomb or when it will detonate.

This frilly red dress with a big white bow tied at the back—a gift from Mariss—does nothing to improve my mood. I keep silent while everyone fawns over me, talking about how adorable I look. Every compliment feels like an insult; I had planned to wear my new romper, but instead I'm here sweating in this potpourri outfit.

Daddy was surprised when I agreed to wear the dress,

along with Mariss's necklace with the spiral pendant, without putting up a fuss. He still doesn't know about the "after dark incident," and maybe before all this my choice of wardrobe would have been a battle worth fighting for. Now I have bigger fish to fry, and I need to keep close watch to find out exactly what kind of fish I'm dealing with.

I focus on Mariss and Daddy in the middle of the dance floor. Of course, Mariss looks dazzling in a simple white-lace wrap dress, with her hair pulled back in a bun. I could swear you aren't supposed to wear white to weddings; I think it's an insult to the bride. Together, they look like the newly married couple.

I shiver in my seat.

Something is different about Daddy . . .

I stare at him, my lips pressed together in concentration. He's changed from his standard stained T-shirt and old jeans to a black tuxedo. He's also gotten a haircut and his beard trimmed.

But it's something else.

I glance at the bride, Ramona. She's busy taking selfies with her bridesmaids. Ramona is one of Miss Mo's many sisters, or is she her cousin? Ahkai's family is so large it's hard to keep track. Apparently, Miss Mo tried to set up Ramona and Daddy when we first moved next door, but I would throw my Barbie doll at Ramona's head whenever she came over. I look at her now, laughing with her new husband, and wonder if it should be my daddy feeding her cake instead.

An old man in a baggy silver three-piece suit hobbles over to Ramona for his photo opportunity, and that's when it hits me.

Daddy no longer walks with the limp!

I try to remember the last time I rubbed Benjie's onto his knee; I had assumed it was just another duty Mariss had taken over, but he is spinning Mariss around on the dance floor and not once doing the inconspicuous foot shake to ease the pressure from his knee.

How could it have healed? I look at the two tiny black lines on my elbows, remembering how quickly my own cuts healed ... *after Mariss touched them with her freaky static electricity!*

A few weeks ago I would've written it off as a coincidence, but after what happened the other night, it's impossible for me to dismiss any strange phenomenon.

Like the frozen cricket ball. The weight on my shoulders feels ten times greater.

Ahkai is next to me, bopping his head to the dancehall beat. He's still a bit annoyed that I stormed into his house the morning after the "after dark incident" to check Simba's breath for a fishy smell, and also his paws for blood or fins. Though I am convinced that Mariss is behind Mr. Pimples's disappearance, I had to eliminate all suspects.

"Ahkai." He doesn't look around. "Have . . . have you ever wondered if, you know, those creatures your mom tells us about—soucouyants, douens, Heartman, you know. You think they could be real?"

Ahkai stops dancing and takes a deep breath. He has about as much tolerance for folklore debates as I have for frilly dresses.

"Not everything about them," I say quickly. "Just one or two things."

Ahkai shakes his head and continues to bounce to the music. At first, I don't think he's going to respond, but then he blurts out: "Of course, some of those characters are derived from facts. I read that the Heartman was based on a real serial killer. Do you know Ossie Moore was a real person? A handyman from Paynes Bay—I really want to dance to this song so be quiet until it's finished."

I want to ask more questions but I hold my tongue. The band ends the song at a crescendo, and the crowd hoots and cheers. All except for the table in front ours, where a group of older women in pastel skirt suits and wide-brimmed hats are busy piling their rice and peas, macaroni pie, sweet potato pie, pudding and souse, peanuts and melon all together in Tupperware containers to take home, before going for second helpings.

We're seated at the kids' table with Ahkai's other cousins, and Daddy, Mariss, and Miss Mo are at the table behind us. I mull over Ahkai's revelations and play with a ribbon-wrapped bar of chocolate, tossing it in the air with one hand. I miss my ball . . .

"Vincent! Josephine? You is a big girl now! Looka you!"

Ramona has reached our table. I give her a polite wave and focus on my chocolate. Ramona plants a kiss on Ahkai, ignoring the fact that he tried to duck. He rubs the red lipstick stain from his cheek.

"Who looking sweet? Who looking sweet?" Miss Mo swings Ramona around, admiring her fitted lace wedding dress. "I tell yuh Shirley is the best needleworker 'bout the place." Miss Mo steps back so Ramona can approve her pink polka-dot outfit.

Ramona's face is flushed—I'm not sure if it's makeup or joy—either way she's shining as bright as the diamantés on her dress. You'd never guess she's my daddy's age; she's not much taller than me, and I'm pretty sure she could fit into my potpourri dress if she wanted to.

"Congrats again, Mona." Dad gives her a hug. Of

course, his shadow, Mariss, has stood up too and is waiting to be acknowledged.

"This is my, uh, partner, Mariss." I press my hand down so hard on the candy bar that chocolate bursts out from the side and stains the tablecloth. *Mariss has been promoted from "friend" to "partner" in six weeks.* Even though Mariss is just meeting Ramona, she pulls her into an embrace like they're long-lost sisters.

"So how wunna meet?" Ramona asks. I perk up in my seat. How *did* they meet? If I knew where Mariss came from, maybe I could figure out her motives . . . and how to get rid of her. Even Miss Mo, who was refolding the napkins on the table, pauses to listen.

"That's a good question," Daddy replies, scratching his chin.

"Welllll," Mariss drawls in her singsong voice reserved for teasing. "I was having an evening swim, and this one here charmed me into walking home with him."

Daddy slaps his forehead. "Oh, right, I got lucky twice that day! The other men ain' get a bite, 'cause you know the fish scarce, but that day my net was full. Then Mariss just seem to rise up out the water like a goddess—"

My eyes widen and chills run down my entire body.

Didn't Daddy tell me about mermaids who comb their

hair by a river? *River Mumma!* That was the name. It was the same day he brought home the brass comb—that wonderful magic comb that cursed knots away! This can't all be a coincidence.

Mariss lets out a throaty laugh, which now sounds like someone blowing bubbles underwater. "You are too much! I felt so drawn to him. We had an amazing connection."

Daddy kisses her on the forehead. I'm shaking so much that the frills on my dress rustle like dry leaves.

"Aww, he's a sweetheart. You're a lucky woman." Ramona is already eyeing the table in front, where a woman in a red hat is beckoning with her Chinese fan.

"I know. And your new husband is very handsome," Mariss replies. "You will make beautiful children."

There is an awkward pause.

"Cheese on bread, now." Miss Mo sucks her teeth and starts fiddling with the napkins again. She mutters under her breath—something about people minding their own business.

Ramona's face sags, and her eyes become dull. She forces a smile and opens her mouth to reply, but she can't seem to get a word out. She swallows and then clears her throat. "Sorry, I have to—" Ramona hurries off and goes over to the other table.

Daddy pulls Mariss back into the chair and leans over to her. I have to strain hard to hear.

"Ramona can't 'ave children," Daddy says in a solemn voice. "She been trying for years."

"Oh my goodness." Mariss slams a hand against her chest so hard it echoes like a popping champagne cork. She looks horrified, as if she'd found out the world was ending tomorrow. She jumps from her seat, attempting to go over to Ramona, but Daddy grabs her hand.

"Don't worry about it now." Daddy makes a "tsk" noise three times. "It's too bad 'cause she did always want a big family."

I realize Ahkai is also listening when he makes two "tsk tsk" noises under his breath.

Mariss raises her voice so I can hear. "We're very lucky to have sweet Josie." She settles down in her seat and reaches out to touch me.

I gasp and duck to the ground, pretending I've dropped something. I have a peek and see that she's still leaning forward but is now sneering at my feet; I was able to ditch the white sandals for my sneakers when no one was paying attention. Mariss runs a finger along her lips, deep in thought, and my eyes widen when I realize there's not even a tiny scar on her hand from Simba's attack.

It's like the incident never happened. Before then, the only thing I'd ever seen Simba attack was a can of tuna. But if Mariss really is some kind of half-fish creature then it makes complete sense. She'd be like a walking seafood tower in Simba's eyes. I'm not sure if Mariss is a River Mumma, but now I'm convinced that she's not human.

Daddy offers his elbow to Mariss when it's their turn to get their meal, and with arms interlocked, they head to the buffet table. I move my chair as far away from Mariss as possible, not taking my eyes off them. What does Mariss want with my daddy? I remember he mentioned something about River Mummas causing boats to crash, but nothing's happened to *Joanne*.

Wait . . . he said something about spells . . . they put spells on fishermen! That would explain why Mariss was able to wake Daddy with a whisper. But a spell for what purpose? I watch Daddy pile his plate full of lettuce, vegetables, and everything green, not leaving room for a speck of beef or ham. I don't understand what master plan requires a purge of red meat, but I have to find a way to get rid of Mariss before Daddy sinks further into her clutches.

I dart my eyes away as Mariss and Daddy return to their table. My gaze lands on Ramona, who's back at the head table, and for some reason, our eyes meet for a second before she looks away. She smiles and nods with her bridesmaids, but her entire demeanor is different. She still laughs at the right times during all the speeches by family and friends, but that light never reappears in her eyes.

Pastor Williams, a highly energetic man with a permanent cheesy grin, comes to the mic. "Thank you all for joining us in this joyous-spirited occasion. Does anyone else in the audience care to impart words of wisdom on this beauteous couple as they embark on the next step of their journey?" He dabs the sweat from his nose before it runs down into his gaping mouth.

To my surprise, Mariss waves at the pastor and strides to the front of the room with confidence. I sit up in my seat, wondering what she has planned for the clueless crowd. There are a few mumbles as she walks to the microphone, and as I thought, a few women look displeased that she's wearing white.

Mariss taps the microphone and jumps when it gives off high, screechy feedback. A few people chuckle in the audience, but Mariss composes herself and straightens her back.

"Thank you, Father." Mariss's voice is soothing on the mic. "Lord be with you."

"And also with you," the crowd responds.

"One word frees us of all the weight and pain of life. That word is 'love.'"

The crowd claps. The red-hat woman beats the fan in front of her face and shouts, "Amen!" Another woman to her left shouts, "Yes, it's true!"

"They say there are plenty of fish in the sea, but only one fish can be your true love. Cherish that love, because it is fragile. Put each other first—always. True love comes before happiness. True love comes before friends. True love even comes before family."

Mariss pauses and stares right at me. The intensity in her eyes sends shivers up and down my spine.

She breaks our gaze. "I'd like to dedicate this song, this song celebrating true love, to the happy couple."

A hush takes over the room when Mariss sings the first note. It is high but gentle, reminding me of "Ave Maria," but there are no words I can understand.

"What's she singing?" I whisper to Ahkai. If anyone could translate mermaid language it would be him. But he ignores me, gawking at Mariss with a dazed expression. In fact, everyone is silent in the hall; even the waiters have stopped serving drinks to listen to her song. If a baby's laugh mixed with a drop of holy water, it could not be as pure and enthralling as Mariss's voice.

Mariss walks over to the head table and touches the front of Ramona's dress, just under the jeweled lining around her waist, and Ramona does not pull away. I look around but no one else seems to think it's strange for Mariss and Ramona to be so engrossed in each other.

Ramona's eyes glisten, and then a tear runs down her cheek. Mariss does a seamless transition into a higher pitch without taking a breath.

This part is familiar...

It's the same weird falsetto that Daddy hums! I glance at him. He's staring at Mariss with that same blank expression.

Wait a minute...

I swerve my head around the room again. All the men have the same empty, fish-eyed look. The women are captivated by Mariss, yes, but on close inspection, their faces are still animated—blinking, smiling, twitching.

Something weird is going on, but before I can process my thoughts, a strange warmth comes over me, and I find it hard not to stare at Mariss. Though the words are foreign, the melody takes me on a journey, a journey from a place of loneliness, through battles, disaster, and suffering, until finally, love and peace. It's like I'm at the cinema, popcorn clenched in my fist, watching an epic movie.

Then, something flutters near my throat and breaks me out of my trance. It's a centipede! I am so terrified of the hundred-legged creatures that the slightest brush on my skin is enough to make me levitate and slap at the area. I've seen strong, able-bodied fishermen dive into the sea to avoid the painful sting from the beasts.

I scratch at my throat and beat on the frills, furious that the centipede has so many hiding places, but nothing falls from the dress. Maybe it was a loose thread . . .

Suddenly, my head is clear. The urgent, compelling notes in Mariss's song return to a pleasant but bland tune, but now I have goose bumps as large as cricket balls.

I think I just got a taste of Mariss's spellbinding powers.

Mariss finishes her last note and there is silence. Then, a thunder of applause. Miss Mo gets to her feet and shouts, "Thank yuh, Jesus!" Not to be outdone, the hat women at the table in front of us jump out of their chairs, raise their hands, and scream, "Hallelujah!" over and over again.

"Whoop! Whoo—" Ahkai stops cheering when he sees the expression on my face. His "whoop" dies and he raises his eyebrow, concerned.

Pastor Williams wipes a tear from his eye. "An angel sings!" he cries into the mic. "Ladies and gentlemen, we are so blessed to have witnessed a true gift from God."

No one cheers louder than Daddy. He meets Mariss on her way back to the table and embraces her. It takes all my strength not to leap to my feet and scream a warning. Pastor Williams signals to the band to start playing a song and invites everyone to dance.

"That was beautiful," says Miss Mo. "I never hear a song like that before. Where it from?"

"It is very old," replies Mariss, avoiding the question. "Pardon, I need to use the restroom." I grimace as she gives Daddy a quick peck on the lips before leaving the table. "Save the next dance for me."

She seems to glide on the varnished floor. Daddy watches her walk away and then turns to me, his eyes bright. "She's wonderful, Bean. I really want you two to get along, please, Bean, for me."

I don't answer. Instead, I pretend to be fascinated with my feet. Ahkai pokes me with a fork and asks me a silent question, but what would I tell him? That I think Mariss is a River Mumma? He'd accuse me of being as kooky as Miss Mo.

Miss Mo!

I whirl around in the chair. She's still at Daddy's table, now scraping leftover food onto one plate. She would know everything about a River Mumma! Didn't she try to warn Daddy when he showed her the comb?

I move to get up from my seat but Miss Alleyne steps behind my chair.

"Ah, the inseparable two." She squeezes my shoulder and waves at Ahkai. It is always strange to see your teacher outside school. Sometimes I forget they don't live there.

Her dreadlocks are twisted on top of her head like an intricate crown. She wears a conservative black dress, but it looks extra fancy, and long beaded earrings that drop past her shoulders.

I mumble a reply, trying to shift out of the seat to reach Miss Mo, but it's too late. She's already disappeared in the crowd with a stack of plates.

I sigh and sit back in the chair, but then I notice Daddy's eyes have bulged out, and he's staring at Miss Alleyne. I understand why when she turns around. The so-called simple dress is backless!

"Hi, you," she says to him with a smile.

"Aurora! 'Ow are you?" Daddy stands to hug her.

A plan forms in my head—Operation Lesser Evil. Maybe Miss Alleyne can distract Daddy from Mariss. If I have to choose between sea creature or teacher, I'll settle for the second option.

"Daddy! You love this song!" I exclaim. I have no idea what the song is, but it sounds close to the ones on the mixed reggae CD Daddy plays on Sunday evenings . . . well, what he used to play on Sunday evenings.

"Let's show these kids how it's done," says Miss Alleyne, holding out her hand. Daddy glances toward the bathroom.

"Go on, Daddy!" I urge. Now there's no way my polite father would refuse.

Daddy gives me a stern look, and I smile my most innocent smile as he holds Miss Alleyne's hand, taking her onto the dance floor. I watch him fumble, trying to find the safest place to rest his hand on her back.

Miss Alleyne says something that makes him laugh. She looks quite pleased with herself and returns his smile with one so genuine it shifts her entire stance. Daddy relaxes and they sway to the song. The band changes the mood to up-tempo oldie goldies—the type of songs the old man selling bread in his white Suzuki van plays from the speakers. They stop swaying, and Daddy does his silly, corny dance that makes me want to disown him.

He looks like a bear stepping on hot coals. Miss Alleyne gapes at him, body poised in her sophisticated-looking dress and silver heels.

I groan. *There goes my plan.*

Then, Miss Alleyne starts to have a seizure! Wait, no,

she's dancing too! Pinching her nose and wiggling up and down.

Ahkai points at them, laughing. Soon, the entire crowd is cheering them on. The bridesmaids, with their high heels in their hands, take to the dance floor and form a conga line. The band starts to play the calypso song "In de Congaline," and suddenly most of the crowd is on the dance floor.

Among the flailing bodies, I notice a rigid one in the corner. The brass pendant gleams in the blue artificial lights.

Mariss.

She glares at Daddy and Miss Alleyne, her eyes so filled with hate I shudder in my seat. I wonder if she's mad enough to make a scene, or worse, attack them on the dance floor. She *was* bold enough to enchant an entire congregation. Who knows what other special powers she has . . . maybe she can turn them into seaweed to blend in one of her awful smoothies?

Mariss marches toward them, and I search the table for a weapon, but I have nothing but a dirty napkin at my disposal.

She pushes between Daddy and Miss Alleyne, and Miss Alleyne steps back, startled. I expect Mariss to swallow her whole, but instead she turns and looks into

Daddy's eyes, moving her ample hips from side to side, out of sync with the upbeat tune. Mariss puts her hands around Daddy's neck, and they start slow dancing, oblivious to everyone else in the room. I'm both relieved and repulsed.

The hall is bursting with dancing bodies, but I have never felt more alone.

It cannot get any worse from here.

Fifteen minutes later, Mariss catches the bride's bouquet.

CHAPTER 13

Mariss is in a white wedding dress, urging Ramona to catch her bouquet. Ahkai is in a black tuxedo that is three sizes too big, officiating the ceremony on the beach.

"Do you, Vincent Cadogan, take Mariss to be your forever companion? Do you promise to love her, in sickness and in health, as long as you both have breath?"

Daddy is like a broken record. "I do I do I do I do I—"

Mariss holds his hand and guides him into the sea, farther and farther, until all that's left is a red wedding veil floating on top of the water.

I jump up in the bed, panting and covered in sweat. I try to go back to sleep, but my stomach feels hard, as if it's filled with cement. I stretch and sit at the window, staring at Miss Mo's house. I wish I had paid more attention to her superstitions instead of dismissing them. I never would have imagined I'd be living with a folklore creature, but if anyone knows how to get rid of a River Mumma, it's Miss Mo.

Finally, her kitchen window slams open. She's up! I race over to the house without bothering to wash my face or brush my teeth.

Miss Mo is bustling about in the kitchen, every burner on the stove occupied.

"I gotta finish cook, then collect donations for the picnic, Jo," Miss Mo announces before I can utter a word, squeezing limes over a bowl of raw chicken.

I forgot about the picnic next weekend. The Fairy Vale Parish Church committee, also known as Miss Mo, voted to have their annual picnic at Brandon's Beach in the city center.

Ahkai enters the kitchen, smiles at me, and grabs a box of cat chow from on top of the fridge. For the first time I'm not happy to see him. If I bring up the River Mumma, he and Miss Mo will no doubt get into another endless argument about myth versus fact.

"Wunna can't go in the Hot Pot, hear?" Miss Mo warns, as if Ahkai and I ever go swimming, much less in the Hot Pot. It's an area off the ocean, a small natural pool at the end of Brandon's Beach.

"Jo, yuh know that water got healing powers, right?" Miss Mo continues. "That's why it so hot."

The water may have healing powers, but it can also be deadly. The Hot Pot is known for its strong rip currents that can drag people out to sea if they're not careful. I grimace, having a flashback to that dreaded day when a silver dollar almost cost me my life.

"Mother." Ahkai grits his teeth. "The Hot Pot is located behind an electrical power station. The hot water from the cooling tanks flowing into the sea is responsible for its warm temperature."

"I had rheumatoid arthritis in my right knee, yuh know. Look!" Miss Mo shouts, pushing a knobbly knee in my face. "One hour in the Hot Pot and all the pain disappear!"

Ahkai closes his eyes and exhales. This is the worst time to talk to Miss Mo but I can't wait any longer.

"Miss Mo, do you know anything about, uh, the . . ." I sit down at the kitchen table, turn away from Ahkai, then whisper, "The River Mumma."

"The River Mumma!" Miss Mo looks like Christmas has come early, and there is an even louder sigh behind me.

I ignore Ahkai. "Yea, uh, her. Does she only live in rivers or what?"

"No, she don't only live in rivers!" Miss Mo lowers the flame underneath the pots. "You can find she in any water, Jo, but she would be called something else. Like some people does call she Mama Dlo, say she is Papa Bois girlfriend, and the fish are her children."

I wonder if this Papa Bois knows Mariss is living with my daddy.

"What does she look like?" I ask. Ahkai gives me his dirty side-eye and shakes cat food into Simba's bowl.

"She ugly, ugly, ugly bad," Miss Mo says, pursing her lips in distaste. "Three red eyes! Mossy teeth and worms for eyebrows! She covers herself with mud and scrubs her armpits with cow-itch."

Ahkai carefully drags a chair across the floor, picks up Simba's food, and leaves the kitchen. I'm pretty sure Miss Mo is describing an alien from a cartoon; I can't believe she's my best source of information, and clearly not a reliable one.

I slump down in disappointment and immediately hear Mariss's voice in my head. *Back straight, shoulders back.* I can't help but spring upright in the chair. Oh man, I need to get her out of my life before she takes over my brain.

"Don't mind he," says Miss Mo. "I know what I telling you. Mama Dlo does get rid of mean-spirited men who harm the trees and forest animals. But you know what to do if you meet she, though."

Miss Mo leans forward and whispers, "Take off yuh right shoe and walk backward till you reach home."

I'm glad Ahkai's not around to hear this. A pot on the stove overflows and Miss Mo hurries to remove the cover. I use the distraction to escape out the kitchen door.

Miss Mo is nuts. If I hadn't witnessed Mariss's spell with my own eyes, her wacky description would make me doubt that creatures like a River Mumma or Mama Dlo exist. But now I'm back to square one, with no idea where to find credible facts. I had put all my hope in Miss Mo.

Though my house is across the street, I feel so lost.

Still, maybe it's possible that some River Mummas have mossy teeth and I was just fortunate to meet one with good hygiene. I have to do something and it can't hurt to try Miss Mo's advice. After checking for incoming vehicles (and Ahkai), I walk across the road backward, with my slipper clenched in my hand. I feel around for the doorknob and back into the hallway.

"Oh, good, you're up!" Mariss exclaims.

Guess that didn't work ...

Having my back to Mariss seems like a bad idea so I spin around and see her at the bottom of the stairs in her red robe and fluffy white slippers.

Now that I know Mariss isn't human, she looks dangerous, even in pajamas. I wait until she's in the kitchen before inching toward the stairs.

"You can help me make pancakes for your daddy before school."

No way I'm going near her, especially in a room full of knives. Mariss moves around the kitchen with ease, her hands now familiar with the location of all the bowls and measuring cups.

"I was thinking we could try some with almond milk and coconut oil!" She claps her hands in excitement. "Maybe even some chia seeds!"

Mariss's smile falters when she sees the disgust on my face.

"Maybe we can add chocolate chips?" Mariss, looking hopeful, holds up a bag of the treats. Nope, not even Hershey's creamy milk chocolate can get me alone in the kitchen with her.

"Oh, good, pancakes for breakfast." Daddy comes down the stairs, rubbing his temples. "I ain' sleep good last night and now my 'ead aches," he groans. "I need some tea."

He kisses me on the head, and then embraces Mariss. She nuzzles his cheek with her nose, but I'm not swayed by her gentle affection. *What does she want with my daddy?* She doesn't belong in my kitchen making pancakes with seeds! I turn away from their gross cuddling and head upstairs.

"Bean." I look back at Daddy. His head is cocked to the side. "Pancakes."

"I'm not hungry," I reply. I can't miss the disappointment in his eyes before I run upstairs and close my bedroom door. I get ready for school, trying to ignore the smell of melted chocolate and the rumbling in my belly. When I'm sure they're both upstairs in their room, I sneak back over to Miss Mo's, hoping she'll have leftovers from breakfast and maybe remember something useful about mythical sea creatures.

Before I can get onto the veranda, the door bursts open. Ahkai rushes toward me so fast that his glasses fall off his face.

"Simba! Simba! Simba! Simba!" Ahkai cries out. "Simba is missing!"

CHAPTER 14

We search for Simba for an hour, looking in all the breadfruit and mango trees in the area. We put fresh tuna in his food dish to make him come out of hiding, but when we return the fish is still there, untouched. Miss Mo isn't happy that we "wasted her good tuna" but even she seems concerned that Simba hasn't been seen since yesterday.

I am convinced that Mariss is responsible for Simba's disappearance, especially after he attacked her, but I have no proof.

I remember the look of controlled rage in Mariss's eyes.

"It's Mariss!" I shout. I look around, and bring my voice to a whisper. "Mariss may be behind all this."

Ahkai frowns. "I do not understand."

I tell him everything, pacing back and forth, details of recent events pouring out of me—the standstill cricket ball, the trances and hypnotic singing, and I remind him about how much Mariss disliked Simba.

I have to catch my breath after my rambling testimony.

"So, Mariss is a sea creature who can manipulate cricket balls, perform hypnosis, and has kidnapped my cat." Ahkai stares at me like he's waiting for the punch line to my joke. I can't blame him; my theory sounds even more ridiculous when spoken out loud.

I need to get proof.

"Maybe Simba is just visiting a friend," Ahkai says, his voice full of misery. "I think I should stay home and wait for him."

You know it's bad when Ahkai wants to skip school and miss reading in the library.

Wait—the library! I should be able to find information about sea creatures in one of those books.

"Ahkai, I think we should go to school and make MISSING posters on the computer."

We head straight to the library after the school bell rings for lunch, and while Ahkai logs onto the computer,

I look around for Mrs. Edgecombe, the librarian. She's nowhere to be seen, or more likely, heard.

Mrs. Edgecombe is the loudest librarian in the world; the students have to ask her to be quiet. She is a heavy-set woman with long Jheri curls that always leave the back of her neck wet and shiny. She wears thick black glasses and has a curved back from all the time she spends folded over with books. Mrs. Edgecombe reacts to reading books like regular people react to watching TV soap operas. Every few minutes, she will shout, burst out laughing, or wail while reading the pages.

Ahkai is her favorite student, and she is his favorite teacher. He even speaks to her sometimes. I admit I get a little jealous when I see them sitting together, sharing a book. Ahkai politely waits for Mrs. Edgecombe to finish the page, and she always asks, "Yuh done?" even though he reads much faster than she does.

Since we don't have a picture of Simba for the poster, we decide to browse the internet to find a tabby that resembles him.

"How about this one?" I ask Ahkai.

"No! Simba is three inches taller than this specimen," snaps Ahkai. "And this cat's fur is Naples yellow, not mustard." He gives me the stink eye.

I sigh. We've been here for forty minutes and all we have is:

MISSING CAT
SIMBA
BDS $100,000 REWARD

I tell Ahkai the reward is too high, but he insists Miss Mo would be willing to sell the house. After a few minutes, I convince him otherwise.

MISSING CAT
SIMBA
~~BDS $100,000 REWARD~~
BDS $1,000 REWARD

Sigh.
After much more convincing:

MISSING CAT
SIMBA
~~BDS $100,000 REWARD~~
~~BDS $1,000 REWARD~~
BDS $10 REWARD

Ahkai's decided to sketch a picture of Simba himself so I take the opportunity to browse the internet for information. I type in "sea creature barbados" but I only get hits about fish and turtles.

There's still no sign of Mrs. Edgecombe so I wander about the library, looking for a section about sea creatures that heal themselves and hate cats . . .

A loud cackle erupts from behind a shelf, and I spy Mrs. Edgecombe hiding at the back of the library, sitting on the carpet and huddled in the corner with a book in her lap.

"Mrs. Edgecombe?"

She tightens her lips and furrows her eyebrows as I try to get her attention. "After this chapter! After this chapter!"

"But, ma'am—"

"Shhhh . . . before they hear you." She gestures to a line of children at her desk, waiting to check out books.

"Ma'am, are there any sea creatures in Bajan folklore?"

Mrs. Edgecombe's eyes dart up from the page. "From the sea? Not really, but . . ." Her bottom lip quivers, like she's fighting to remain silent, but in the end she can't resist the urge to tell a story. "There's the Mami Wata, a powerful water goddess," she finally replies, her voice just above a whisper and a wild gleam dancing in her eyes.

"The Mami what?"

Mrs. Edgecombe adjusts her glasses and recites information like she's in a trivia tournament. "River Mumma, Mere de l'eau, Mama Dlo, all these manifestations originate from the Mami Wata in African mythology, and often take on characteristics unique to the region or culture. For instance, in some interpretations they could look like a mermaid, with a bottom half like a fish, but in others, the bottom half could be like a snake."

I'm glad there's some truth to Miss Mo's information, and it seems more valid coming from Mrs. Edgecombe.

"They're healers—not just of physical pain. They can even cure infertility and emotional suffering." Mrs. Edgecombe taps on her chest. "They restore that spiritual balance inside. That's why they're respected, adored, loved by so many! They take care of those who worship them. A provider of riches!"

I think about our fully paid bills, our new window, new Jalopy, Daddy's nets full of fish . . . Mrs. Edgecombe is too engrossed in her storytelling to notice my growing dread.

She cocks her head to the side. "Now that I think 'bout it, a Bajan Mami Wata would be . . . a kind of Sea Mumma. I wonder what they'd be like. Everyone—even deities—has different personalities."

Yes, they could like pancakes with seeds and hate bad posture.

Mrs. Edgecombe wags her finger in my face. "And don't piss them off, hear? Every coin has two sides! Like all powerful creatures, they are as dangerous as they are generous. They could bewitch people, yes? Possess them in their dreams. Bad things happen to people who anger them."

I struggle to breathe as I remember Daddy's nightmare where he saw fangs . . . and Mariss's rage when she saw Daddy and Miss Alleyne dancing. My body aches for air, but I can't seem to inhale.

There's no doubt in my mind that Mariss is a Sea Mumma.

"What do they want from people, ma'am?" I manage to gasp. "Our organs? Our *soul*?"

"They're spirits, not demons, Josephine." Mrs. Edgecombe huffs as if I've offended her in some way. "Most of the time people want things from them, except if . . ." Her voice trails away and Mrs. Edgecombe lowers her eyes to the page, distracted by the text.

"Except if what, ma'am?" I ask, putting my hand over the page.

Mrs. Edgecombe swats me away like I'm a mosquito. "Except if . . . they choose someone as a mate . . . but that only happens once . . . in a lifetime. Now go away, Josephine."

I start trembling. *Not my daddy.*

"What happens to the person she chooses as a mate? How do you get rid of a Sea Mumma, ma'am?" I ask quickly. I'm desperate for info, and Mrs. Edgecombe will soon be lost in her book again.

"I dunno, you know. Most books just warn people to stay away."

"Please, ma'am!" I raise my voice.

Mrs. Edgecombe gets up with another huff and pulls a heavy book from a nearby shelf. The words "*The Treasure Chest of African and Caribbean Folklore*" shine in gold letters on the cover.

"There may be something in this book, but it's the only copy. If I let you borrow it, will you leave me alone?"

It takes all my self-control not to snatch the book out of her hands. I need to find out how to get rid of Mariss. Plus, Ahkai is more likely to believe me if I can get information from a printed source.

I wait in the line with the other children, and after Mrs. Edgecombe allows me to check out the text, she returns to the corner with her book and pushes her head down into her collar like a turtle.

I flip through the pages. There are blue ink scribbles in the margins, as if someone tried to update the text. Most of the handwriting is unintelligible; in fact, I don't recognize any of the words. Yet while the pages have yellowed with age, the printed text is still clear.

There's no table of contents or index, but as I settle to read from the first page, Ahkai ambles over with a stack of papers. He holds up a flyer with Simba's drawing, trying to hold back tears.

I can't let him down so I spend the rest of lunchtime with Ahkai, passing around copies of the flyer, and after school Miss Mo drives us all around Fairy Vale, helping us stick them on every wall and pole.

As soon as we get home, I leap out of her car, eager for the first time to read a book. I'm prepared to spend all night reading until I find the information I need.

"Mariss?" Daddy calls from the kitchen.

"It's me, Daddy."

Should I tell him that he's dating a sea spirit? I remember Ahkai's skeptical face and hide the book in my bag, deciding to wait until I have solid proof.

Daddy is at the table with bills. I haven't seen him in this position in so long that for a second I think my wish has come true, and we've gone back to a time when Mariss wasn't in our lives, and my only challenge was getting on the cricket team. I throw myself over him, giving him the biggest of hugs, then squeeze onto his chair and reclaim my rightful place on his chest.

"What is organic greens powder?" he asks, bringing me closer. "And why I paying over a 'undred dollars for it? And the electricity and water bills triple! This ain' make no sense to me."

"No bite today?" I ask. He has the worried crease in his forehead.

"You not gine believe this, but only one fish. One single fish. I don't understand it. The other fishermen ain' had no problems," he says, shaking his head from side to side. "It was like *Joanne* had on some kinda fish repellent."

Mariss's words are burned into my memory: *There are plenty of fish in the sea, but only one fish can be your true love.* I can't forget the fury on Mariss's face while she watched Daddy dancing with Miss Alleyne yesterday. Now after weeks of good fortune, Daddy wakes up with head pains, and his nets are empty. Is this some kind of warning?

I've got a bad feeling about this.

"Hang in there, Daddy. It always works out," I say, trying to cheer him up. "Remember that time I broke the window, and we had no idea how we would get it fixed?"

"Mmm," Daddy replies.

"And remember the time Jalopy broke down, and we had no idea how we would find the money for a new engine?"

"True." Daddy nods his head.

"And remember the time you didn't think you could afford a laptop for your lovely daughter's birthday next week, but then you bought it anyway?"

Daddy sucks his teeth, but starts to laugh. "I dunno what to do with you." He tickles me under my ribs.

The tickle! Oh, how I've missed the tickle!

I don't bother to pretend I want him to stop. But then, I notice a dark mark peeking out from under his shirt.

"Daddy, what's that?" I pull down his shirt collar. On his chest, just above his heart, is a tattoo of a spiral.

"What?" Daddy says, fixing his shirt.

"That tattoo," I say, jabbing his chest. "Did you get that for Mariss?" It's shaped exactly like her spiral pendant.

"Stop playing!" Daddy laughs and tries to tickle me again, but I push him away. He's marked his skin with Mariss's design, like some kind of lovesick tribute. I have to warn him now before I come home from school and find them married.

"Daddy, I don't think Mariss is who she says she is."

"What you talking 'bout now, Josephine?"

"I think Mariss is a creature from the sea—"

"Enough, Josephine, enough! I tired of you making so much trouble." He gets to his feet, and his features are twisted in so much anger he's almost unrecognizable. "I normally turn a blind eye to your bad behavior, but I'm putting my foot down! I don't want to 'ear another negative word about Mariss. She is 'ere FOR GOOD!"

I jump up as Daddy crashes his hand onto the table and shatters a small plate. I back away, and he stares at his fist as if surprised by his own actions. A tiny piece of ceramic drops off the table and bounces just shy of my foot.

My daddy has never lost his temper like this—not ever. He's changing . . . like he's being possessed!

He doesn't apologize or rush to clean up the shards; in fact, he doesn't look at me. Instead, Daddy clears his throat, pushes the broken pieces aside, and then stares off into the distance as if nothing happened.

I rush upstairs, determined to read every single word of this book until I find a way to get rid of Mariss.

I almost lost Daddy once. I won't let it happen again.

CHAPTER 15

My eyes burn as I read the folklore book, scanning the long chunks of paragraphs and small print. I have to force myself not to skip ahead, in case I miss the one line that could reveal how to get rid of Mariss. I so wish Ahkai could help because he's a much faster reader, but he's not in a place to help anyone . . . even me.

It's been twelve days and Simba still hasn't come home.

Waiting for news with Ahkai was almost unbearable, with him stationed by the phone. But that was nothing compared to his sullen depression when he began to lose hope. Miss Mo keeps fussing over him, forcing him to swallow raw aloe and rubbing him down in coconut oil. Between being worried about him and Daddy, it's tougher to get through the heavy text than I imagined.

Mariss's spiral pendant on my dresser gleams in the sunrise.

I need more time to find out what she wants and how to get rid of her. I've avoided her as much as I could, but I can't maintain that behavior without upsetting Daddy. He keeps trying to get us to spend time together and hinted that we're going to "spend time as a family" for my birthday tomorrow.

I've never been less excited. I know he expects me and Mariss to become best friends.

That's when it hits me.

Maybe I can make Mariss *think* that we're friends, so I can figure out her motives, once and for all. Today is the picnic at Brandon's Beach and it's the perfect opportunity to get closer to her. I push the book under my pillow and look at my reflection in the mirror; I think I can act like a friendly almost-eleven-year-old girl.

Miss Mo organized a park and ride to the beach, so everyone has to gather at Fairy Vale Academy, then board a shuttle bus to the city. When I get downstairs, Daddy's already dressed in swim trunks and a sleeveless shirt, but the spiral tattoo on his chest isn't visible. Mariss walks out of the kitchen with a large container of salad.

She immediately notices the necklace around my neck. "I knew you'd like it! You just had to give it a chance."

I smile so hard that my eyes become tiny slits and she is a blur. I force myself to stay still as Mariss comes over and presses her cheek to mine. "Look Vincey, we're twins!" she says, pointing to our matching necklaces.

"We're so totally alike," I respond, hoping my disgust isn't evident.

"My girls!" Daddy beams at us. When Mariss turns away, Daddy mouths "thank you." This is one of the hardest things I've ever done—much, *much* harder than solving fractions.

I am excited to see Ahkai with Miss Mo at the meeting point, standing in line next to the shiny blue-and-yellow Transport Board bus that looks new, but chugs like an old locomotive. He refuses to talk to anyone, but when I sit next to him, I can tell he's glad I'm there.

The bus is jam-packed, with people squeezed against coolers and beach chairs and trying to hold on to handrails and food containers without falling. Still, it's a bright day with a cool morning breeze, so everyone is cheerful enough to join in when Mariss initiates one of those horrid sing-alongs.

As soon as we arrive at the beach, Daddy races across the long stretch of white sand and dives into the clear blue-green waters. Mariss throws her head back and cackles at his childish joy, the amber highlights in her hair catching the sunlight. For a split second, I get the urge to laugh with her. I shake off the feeling and plaster a fake smile on my face. "So, do you have any brothers or sisters?"

"No, Josie, it's just me," Mariss replies, helping a lady with a newborn off the bus.

"Not anymore!" I exclaim in an extra chirpy voice. Mariss looks pleased.

"And no kids?" I ask later, when she's changing the baby's diaper on a blanket under the almond trees.

"No, Josie Sweets . . . not yet," she responds, with a small smile that makes my skin crawl.

I finally manage to wrangle some personal information out of her while we're putting coals in the barbecue grill.

"How did you come up with this design?" I ask, dusting specks of sand off the pendant.

Mariss straightens the pendant, her fingernails brushing against my chest. I try not to flinch. "It's my family symbol, and this particular piece is a treasure." Then, with a faraway look in her eyes, she continues, "It's a tribute to my great-great-grandmother."

I want to pry further, but Coach Broomes interrupts our conversation. I've managed to avoid him since the friendly match, but now it's too late to run away.

He wears a white T-shirt and colorful swim trunks, and a pained grimace on his face. At first I wonder if he's about to confirm I didn't make the team, but then I realize he's smiling. It's like he needed to spray lubricant onto his face to revive the muscles. Even worse, he looks unbalanced and incomplete without his clipboard.

"Josephine, yuh ain' tell me you had such a lovely sister," says Coach Broomes in an extra deep voice. I am so confused. One—it's odd to hear Coach Broomes say my name without frustration. Two—he knows I'm an only child. Three—those swim trunks are wayyyy too short.

"This is my, uh, my, uh, friend, Mariss." I choke out the words while looking at the sky, the grill, anywhere but at Coach Broomes's hairy thighs.

Mariss giggles and draws me closer. "Why, I'm practically Josie's stepmom."

I close my eyes and count to ten. My mouth quivers from the effort to maintain my smile and hold in my outburst. *Do not offend her . . .*

"Mariss! How are you?" Miss Alleyne walks up to the gathering, carrying a large black bag and looking fantastic in an African-print dashiki. Her dreadlocks are pulled back into a loose ponytail.

"Aurora!" Mariss meets Miss Alleyne halfway and they embrace like they're old friends.

My mouth falls open. I will never understand adults. Maybe they're both pulling a similar ruse. Being extra sweet to each other to get information.

I have to be patient. Eventually, Mariss will show her true intentions. Soon, Daddy will see the truth for himself.

"Come help me set up for volleyball." Miss Alleyne grabs Mariss's hand, and I follow them down the beach, toward Ahkai, who is whittling on a blanket a little ways off from the main activity.

Mariss and Miss Alleyne are pounding a stake into the sand with a rock when Coach Broomes approaches.

"Lemme help you with this before yuh hurt yourself," he says, reaching for the rock. Mariss looks up at him, smiling, and steps aside, but Miss Alleyne waves him away.

"It's a rock, not a bomb." Miss Alleyne laughs and looks over at Mariss for support, but her laughter fades when she sees the baffled look on Mariss's face.

I watch as Coach Broomes and Miss Alleyne's argument somehow escalates into the challenge of a beach volleyball match—men versus women. Instead of playing, Mariss relaxes on a sun lounger like a tourist to observe the game.

Miss Alleyne pulls the dashiki over her head and

throws it to the side. The matching one-piece swimsuit reveals athletic, toned legs. Daddy does a double take, but then looks away, pretending there is something interesting behind him. Mariss sits up in the lounge chair.

Uh-oh. I can't afford for Mariss to get upset in any way. Daddy's finally sleeping well again, and yesterday he got a decent catch in his nets. I remember Mrs. Edgecombe's wagging finger: *Don't piss them off, hear?*

Daddy serves the ball.

"YAH!" Miss Alleyne smacks the ball over the net. Daddy is shocked when the ball flies past him like a rocket.

The women cheer, and Miss Alleyne gives Coach Broomes a triumphant look. Coach Broomes narrows his eyes. He hates to lose. Trust me, he's been kicked off several cricket fields protesting umpire decisions.

It's an intense game. I'm surprised Coach Broomes and Miss Alleyne don't bare their teeth at each other. Daddy, the eternal mediator, is trying his best to stay between them. They're flinging their bodies in the air, desperate to win a point. The score is neck and neck, until Daddy misses Miss Alleyne's return and the women get the final point.

Coach Broomes scowls and kicks the sand in anger. Miss Alleyne's teammates scream out in glee and hug one another and I can't resist joining the celebration.

Mariss gets up from the lounger to comfort Daddy.

"Chin up, Vincent! Come and soak those old bones in the Hot Pot," Miss Alleyne gloats. She's not humble in victory. "Maybe the water will cure those bad reflexes."

"Good game, Aurora." Daddy holds out his hand. He's looking at her the same way he looks at other fishermen when they dock with a boat full of fish; it's a grudging respect. Miss Alleyne flushes and returns his handshake.

Mariss's face is a mixture of rage and confusion, and as seconds pass by and their hands remain intertwined, her lips curl and her expression grows more thunderous. I get an overwhelming urge to yank Daddy and Miss Alleyne apart.

"Miss Alleyne!" I shout. "Come pick sea grapes with me." I point at the trees at the end of the beach, laden with the sweet purple fruit.

Miss Alleyne lets go of Daddy's hand and wipes her hand across her face. "Thanks, Jo, but I need to cool down." She throws her wrap over her shoulder and walks away.

I exhale and feel the need to escape. It's exhausting to keep the peace.

Ahkai's still focused on his new creation, and though he doesn't look up, I know he's aware of the situation. I walk toward the sea grape trees, and a few seconds later I hear him coming behind me.

I pry some of the green, unripe sea grapes from the tube-shaped, hanging bunch of fruit, while Ahkai follows a pigeon through the trees. I bowl the small grapes into a tree branch, trying to hit a black smudge.

"YAH!" I pretend that I'm Miss Alleyne, slamming the ball over the net. The fruit lands squarely in the black area.

Coach Broomes was wrong! Girls can play with boys—and we can win too.

Then, a bloodcurdling scream penetrates the air. My heart stops.

Ahkai!

Thankfully, he bursts out from behind a tree, his eyes wide and filled with fear.

The person screams again. Ahkai and I whip around to our right.

It's coming from the Hot Pot.

My brain tells me to get back to the campsite, but the anguish in that cry is so terrible my heart cannot ignore it.

"Get help!" I tell Ahkai before dashing through the bushes toward the area.

Maybe someone is being pulled out to sea, but it can't be. No one knows better than me that there's no way to scream when you're drowning. Drowning doesn't look like how it does on TV, where a person is splashing and screaming for help. Not when you're trying to avoid swallowing seawater and struggling to breathe.

It is a slow, quiet death.

The Hot Pot is ahead. The strong current pulls the water from the inlet into the ocean. The strength of the water has shifted the sand so it surrounds the pool like a cliff. The rushing water is as loud as rain beating on a rooftop.

I am so blinded by fear that I almost miss the figure floating facedown in the water.

Miss Alleyne!

"Ma'am! Ma'am!" I scream, though I know she won't answer. I look around for help. It's noon—the hottest time of day; everyone is sheltering under the trees farther up on the beach.

I'm all alone.

Miss Alleyne is motionless and her body is heading out to sea. I take a step toward the rushing water. She's about ten feet away. I need to jump in now to catch her or try to block her body from going out to sea.

My toe touches the water and I yelp, jumping back like it's lava.

Get in, Jo! I order myself.

Splash.

I duck as a black-and-brown lionfish leaps out of the water like a flying fish. Its venomous spikes along its spine and around its mouth are stiff and pointed. It glides through the air over Miss Alleyne's body, then turns toward me, its stern face daring me to jump into the pool, before disappearing into the water.

I drop to my knees, a chill sweeping through my body. It's not possible. Lionfish live on the reef under the sea. *And lionfish don't jump.*

Yet, here it is, flipping over her body like an acrobat in a deadly circus act. Distraught, I watch as Miss Alleyne floats past me.

SPLASH!

Daddy has leapt over my head and jumped into the water. All of a sudden, I'm surrounded by people.

"Daddy!"

"Vincey! Don't!"

Then, he disappears underwater.

Every second he is out of sight feels like an hour. I stop hearing the cries around me; there's only the rhythm of my heartbeat ripping through my chest.

After what feels like forever, Daddy appears next to Miss Alleyne. I would collapse if not for Mariss's support. He flips Miss Alleyne onto her back, and using one arm, he struggles to get back to shore. It's like trying to push through a brick wall with one hand. Every time they get a little closer, the current pulls them back out to sea.

I hold on to Mariss, screaming as Daddy fights with the water.

Then, I feel the heat emanating from her body. My scream turns into a gasp—the blood rushes through her veins like running water. *Is she going to turn into a mermaid right here in front of everyone?* I don't dare let go of her waist. I don't want any movement to startle her if she's trying to save my daddy.

Suddenly, the choppy water gets calm, like a vacuum in the sky has sucked all energy from the sea. I let go of Mariss and jump up and down on the beach, shouting words of encouragement to Daddy as he cuts through the still waters. He stumbles to the shore with Miss Alleyne in his arms and collapses onto the sand.

People crowd around us. I cradle Daddy's face in my lap as he catches his breath. Mariss tries to touch him, but I shove her away.

"I good, Bean. I good." Daddy props up on his elbows and crawls over to Miss Alleyne.

Everyone watches, praying for some sign of life as Miss Alleyne, lying motionless on the sand, receives CPR.

"Anybody call fuh the ambulance?" shouts Miss Mo, gently rubbing the top of Ahkai's head. He's hiding his face in his hands.

Gradually, the crowd starts to recount the sequence of events. Ahkai burst into the campsite, frantic but unable to say a word. It was only when Miss Mo returned from the bathroom that Ahkai was able to talk and tell her what had happened.

Miss Alleyne still isn't responding to the CPR. The ground doesn't open up and swallow me whole, so I'm forced to watch and wonder if I could have saved her had I been a little braver. I squeeze Ahkai's hand, and he turns toward me. His eyes are red and full of tears.

I know he's wondering the same thing about himself . . .

He buries his face in Miss Mo's dress and I look away. I've never even seen them hug before, and for once, I feel like an intruder in their personal space.

I turn to Daddy, still pumping on Miss Alleyne's chest, and my eyes are drawn to his bare chest, where the spiral tattoo is pronounced, even on his dark skin. Except . . . I lean in close . . . it's not a tattoo. It's a *burn*. Daddy's been branded, like a cow.

Without thinking, I grab the spiral pendant, yank it until the chain snaps, and fling it out of my hands. It lands in the sea foam at the edge of the breaking waves; the current has returned to full strength and seems to slap the shore in punishment.

I look at Mariss, assuming she'll be focused on Daddy, but instead she's squatting on the sand, trying to catch her breath like she's just run a marathon.

I follow her eyes up to my throat, and I can't help but touch the empty area by my neck.

Oh no . . . I threw away her special treasure.

I rush to get the pendant, but it's too late. The fierce tide covers the jewelry, and it would be so easy to pluck it out of the wave, but I can't bring myself to touch the water.

The tide goes back out, taking the pendant with it. Mariss watches it disappear, and her face crumples like a piece of paper. She reaches her hand out toward the ocean, but nothing happens. The sea remains rough; the only salt water she now controls is the tear running down her cheek. She drops onto the sand and shoves her hands in her hair in angst.

Guilt runs through me. Mariss just saved Daddy's life—I don't know how, but it was her—and I repay her by throwing away her special gift.

Mariss slowly gets to her feet, trembling, and wipes the tear away. Then she turns to me with clenched fists, breathing so hard I can almost see smoke coming from her nostrils. Her anger seems to pull all the heat from the air, and I shiver, wrapping my hands around my body.

She marches away and I take a step after her, but then decide not to follow.

I still don't know what Mariss really wants, but it's clear she genuinely cares about my daddy. It's also clear she has the power to get rid of anyone who pisses her off.

After today, I'm worried the next person on her list is me.

CHAPTER 16

I tried to tell one of the paramedics about the lionfish, but he didn't believe me.

"There aren't any lionfish in this area," he said, "and they live on the reef." Then he looked around at the crowd. "Did anyone else see what happened?"

He was right. Normal lionfish don't go near the Hot Pot, and they also don't jump. But I've seen Mariss somehow control the seawater—it's not far-fetched that she controls the fish in the sea too. Then I remembered Miss Mo's belief that the fish are these creatures' children. Mariss *must* have sent the lionfish to attack Miss Alleyne after the volleyball match . . . and I may be her next victim.

Daddy insisted on riding in the ambulance with Miss

Alleyne, so Mariss and I are alone in the house, waiting for him to return. I shut and lock my bedroom door for the first time, but I am still very aware of her presence.

She walked right past me on the bus, not even sparing a look. I should go apologize—now more than ever, I have to stay on her good side until I can find out how to get rid of her, but I'm nervous and scared. I'm haunted by images of Daddy disappearing under a wave, Miss Alleyne floating facedown in the water, Mariss's tear . . .

When Daddy gets home from the hospital, he tells me Miss Alleyne is still alive, but in a coma. "Nobody ain' know when she gine wake up," he says in a tired voice. "All we can do is pray."

I stay up all night reading again, desperate for new information. So far I know Mariss has the power to put people into trances, heal bruises, and control the seawater and fish, though I still don't know how she stopped a cricket ball in midair. But none of these things reveal how to get rid of her.

When I check the time, it is after five in the morning and I still haven't learned anything new about Sea Mummas. I feel so hopeless; there has to be another way to discover Mariss's weaknesses.

I drag myself downstairs to make some bay leaf tea, and to my surprise, Daddy and Mariss are both sitting at the dining table. No one utters a word; there's just the sound of breathing and spoons clinking on ceramic bowls. It's clear they've been arguing.

"Morning, Bean," Daddy says with zero enthusiasm.

"Good morning, Josephine."

What? No Josie Sweets? I'm not sure how to react. Last week I would have given my two front teeth to get Mariss to call me by my birth name. Now I look at her blank, straight face and dread fills my belly.

I still have to apologize. I don't want her to hurt anyone else.

Daddy rolls the wrinkled sleeves of his shirt over his elbows and he brushes Mariss's black jewelry case by mistake. Mariss gives him a side-eye and moves the case from the table to the ground.

"There's breakfast in the kitchen," says Daddy.

I hurry away, glad for a reason to escape the tension, and notice a big two-layer chocolate cake with pink frosting on the counter.

I scratch my cheek and rub my eyes. Why is there cake for breakfast?

"Happy birthday!" Daddy shouts.

I can't believe I forgot my birthday. Daddy and Mariss sing the happy birthday song but I barely hear them. Mariss has sucked all the joy out of my life; she's consumed my thoughts so much that even now, I don't feel an ounce of excitement for my special day.

"Now, Bean, I didn't get the laptop," Daddy says, placing a hand on my cheek. "But it's the first thing I gine buy when I get a little extra."

I nod, not wanting to hurt his feelings.

"And today, guess where we going?" Daddy is so excited he doesn't wait for me to guess. "The zoo!"

"Zoo?" Mariss and I say at the same time.

"Well, the Wildlife Reserve," says Daddy. "I know you love animals, and it would cheer up Ahkai."

I sigh. I'm not in the mood to celebrate, and I'm not sure Ahkai will want to come with us, even if it's my birthday. Being around all those animals will no doubt remind him of Simba. I had Mr. Pimples for a little over three years, and I still can't bring myself to change the water.

Daddy squeezes my shoulder. "I know it's tough, especially after what 'appen yesterday, but this is a reminder to celebrate life when you can."

"What kind of life is that?" We both turn to Mariss in surprise. "I hate to see poor animals trapped in cages. It's—it's barbaric and cruel! How would *you* feel if your freedom was just taken away?"

I've never seen her so flustered. Now I definitely want

to go to the Wildlife Reserve. Maybe she has a deathly fear of green monkeys . . .

"Sisi." Daddy puts an arm around her shoulder. "It's a reserve. They're free to walk around everywhere."

"Walk around? You know I have allergies." Mariss strokes Daddy's beard. "Can't we just carry a nice packed lunch to the park?"

"Just take an antihistamine. We'll go to Farley Hill tomorrow, just the two of us." Daddy gives her a kiss on the cheek and then shakes out his leg. His knee is acting up again.

"You don't have to come if you don't want to," I say, making an effort to show support, but she ignores me.

"Bean masala for breakfast?" she asks, tightening her robe. My stomach churns at the thought of another portion of tasteless soya chunks.

I look at Daddy with pleading eyes. "Can we have real pancakes, please, Daddy?" I miss Sunday morning pancakes, made with cassava flour and cinnamon.

To my surprise, Daddy agrees. "Sisi, just do the masala for yourself. Bean and I will 'ave pancakes."

Excited, I turn to get ingredients before he changes his mind, but I stop in my tracks when I see Mariss's face. It has not changed, but now her dark brown eyes are light brown, with flecks of green.

I back into the kitchen, feeling along the counter for a weapon, not wanting to take my eyes off Mariss. I still don't know the full extent of her powers so I have to move with caution. My roving hand stumbles upon a wooden handle.

"Knife?"

I jump when Mariss holds out her hand, and my fingers close around the butcher knife. With a cold smile, Mariss twirls an onion in her other hand.

"Can you pass the knife?" Mariss repeats.

Before I can respond, Daddy pulls the knife from my hand and gives it to Mariss. Then he hums and gathers the ingredients for pancakes, blind to the uneasiness in the room. I breathe out when Mariss starts to chop the onion, and attempt to help Daddy while keeping out of her way.

"This is my mom's recipe." I try to make conversation as a kind of peace offering. "With a secret ingredient."

"I can keep a secret," Mariss says, pushing the chopped onion aside. A tiny smile breaks through her icy demeanor.

Why did I say that? I pretend to focus on cracking the eggs. I'm trying to be apologetic, but I'm not ready to share so much yet.

"Well, you tell me, then," Mariss says to Daddy after I

refuse to respond. I tense up, knowing he will spill the beans.

Daddy laughs and ruffles my hair. "I'm sure Bean will tell you eventually." I relax, surprised that he hasn't given away our secret.

BOOM! Mariss slams the knife onto the chopping board, and I dive to the floor, taking the carton of eggs with me. Her force was so strong that the blade is lodged inside the wood.

"Sisi, everything okay?" Daddy asks, concerned. I stay perfectly still. I'm within range of the knife. I'm taking no chances.

Mariss forces a smile. "Just a little tired. Been exerting myself . . . giving a lot."

"Come sit down." Daddy pulls out a stool at the bar. I scramble to my feet, sliding on the slimy egg yolks.

"I need a bath," replies Mariss. She pulls the knife out of the board with ease and then slips out of the kitchen. I expect Daddy to go after her, but he shrugs and continues to mix the batter.

After hearing the bathroom door slam, I calm down and start to clean the mess on the floor. I don't remember the last time Daddy and I were able to spend time alone. I want to ask everything and say nothing all at once.

All of a sudden, I remember one of Jared's Ossie Moore jokes.

"Daddy, Ossie Moore was fishing with a friend, when the boat suddenly caught a leak and started to sink. Ossie Moore jumped overboard, leaving behind his friend, who couldn't swim."

I pause. Daddy's already smiling in anticipation of the punch line.

He's such a nerd.

I miss him.

"Ossie Moore, exhausted from the swim, pulled himself on shore and said, 'Good, I save myself . . . now to go back and save he.'"

Daddy roars with laughter, banging the kitchen counter with his fist. His delight shoves my angst aside and I burst into giggles.

"Thanks, Daddy," I say when we've composed ourselves. I add vinegar to the evaporated milk to make buttermilk.

"For what?"

"For not telling Mariss about the cinnamon."

"Cinnamon?" Daddy stops slicing the bananas.

"Mum's secret ingredient." I shoot him a look of disbelief. *I can't believe he forgot.*

Daddy shakes his head. "No, Bean, it isn't just cinnamon. The secret ingredient is nutmeg."

What?

Daddy massages his forehead. "No wonder it taste different . . . I just thought . . ." Daddy's voice trails off, and his eyes get the glassy look.

"Come back, Daddy, please." I want to know more but I'm scared of losing him.

Daddy looks down at me, puzzled. "I ain' going nowhere, Bean." He kisses me on the forehead, and continues to slice the fruit.

"I met your mum in Grenada, at a food festival. All the food stalls 'ad to feature nutmeg in the dishes, and she bake a red snapper in coconut milk. I can still taste it," he says, smacking his lips. "I 'ad to meet the chef."

I am bursting with excitement from this new information. "Mum was a chef?"

Daddy looks at me, eyebrows furrowed. "I thought you know that!" Before I can answer, he says to himself, "Then again, 'ow could you?"

Daddy sighs and tilts his head to the ceiling. Then he laughs.

"What? What?" I ask, eager to hear more.

"Your mum taught me everything. Before I met her, I

could barely cook the fish I catch. One time, I remember trying to make fish soup. Don't ask me 'ow yuh does burn soup." He laughs again and I laugh with him.

"And your mum looooved dumplings. Even more than me!"

"But Daddy, you don't love dumplings." If he loves dumplings, why does he insist on having only one at a time?

"Bean, nobody could come between your mum and dumplings! I used to take one and leave the rest for 'er." Daddy shrugs his shoulders. "I guess I never 'ad the 'eart to take more after she, you know . . ." he says, his voice trailing off again. He gives the batter a taste.

I am stunned. I might as well have been told I was adopted.

Daddy and I reach for the nutmeg at the same time. He smiles and gestures for me to shake the spice into the batter. Then, he scoops the batter into the frying pan.

"You know she used to play squash?" Daddy continues. "And was real competitive! Never backed down from a challenge. Even travel to St. Lucia to represent Barbados."

I must get my love for sports from Mum as well as Daddy! Warmth spreads through my chest at the thought of her slamming a ball into the air. I try to remember the list of questions I had for Mum for when I see her in heaven, but none come to mind, so I stay quiet, listening to Daddy talk about her. All his memories become my own.

Daddy puts a pancake on a plate and squirts maple syrup on top. "Taste this."

I close my eyes and put a forkful into my mouth. As I chew, I get a clear image of my mummy, her hair pulled back in a messy bun, wearing a dirty yellow apron. She is laughing—I can hear it! It's like a guffaw, a wheeze, one of those laughs that goes in and out as the person catches their breath.

My eyes burn, and it becomes difficult to breathe through my nose.

"Good?" Daddy asks, waiting for my feedback.

I nod and put another piece of pancake into my mouth. It tastes like home. I close my eyes again, hoping to jolt another memory.

Being able to spend the morning with my daddy, eating pancakes and learning about my mummy—this is the birthday present I didn't know I wanted.

CHAPTER 17

To my surprise, Miss Mo tells us Ahkai will come to the Wildlife Reserve. Before heading to his house, I pause at Mr. Pimples's empty tank, wrinkling my nose at the mossy water. I poke the overturned shipwreck, part of me still hoping that Mr. Pimples is playing a champion game of hide-and-seek.

The boat shifts to the side, and I notice something trapped underneath it. It's transparent, and floating, like a jellyfish tentacle.

Is it a piece of plastic bag? Some moss?

I bring my face closer and plunge my hand into the tank. I tug on it but it doesn't budge; it's like it's glued on to the ship. This thing is stronger than it looks. I yank at the tentacle so hard that I fall over and hit into one of the stools.

"Bean?" Daddy calls from upstairs.

I rush through the door, twirling the tentacle around my finger, examining its diamond-like pattern, and shove it in my pocket.

Ahkai is sitting at the kitchen table, focused on Miss Mo yapping on the phone. He jumps up when he notices me, his eyes bright and full of life. I never thought I'd see him looking happy again so soon. I fight the urge to throw my arms around him.

"Miss Alleyne woke up!" he cries. It's the first time he's spoken to me in days.

Yes! Relief rushes through me.

Ahkai and I stare at each other with goofy smiles and clear consciences. It almost feels like all is right with the world again.

"I can't believe it! Lionfish don't attack nobody. She had to accidentally step on a dead one."

Lionfish?

Miss Mo notices me gawking at her and pulls the receiver from her ear. "Jo! Miss Alleyne say she get sting by lionfish and couldn't move she body. I can't believe it."

Ahkai clarifies for me, "The venom from the fish spine causes temporary paralysis and extreme pain."

"Tell the doctor boil some soursop leaves and give she to drink," Miss Mo instructs the person on the line.

I don't gloat about being right or point out that nobody listened to me. Mariss has to be stopped, and I can't do it alone.

I gesture for Ahkai to follow me outside into the yard, and I pull the tentacle from my pocket.

"What's this?" I ask him. "I found it in Mr. Pimples's tank."

Ahkai examines it, rubbing the tentacle between his fingers. "I am not sure. It feels scaly."

"It's evidence! That's what it is."

Silence.

I plead my case again. "You know it's not logical for lionfish to be in the Hot Pot."

Ahkai nods. "The heated temperature in the Hot Pot alone *should* deter them from that environment."

"Bad things happen to people who Mariss hates." I fill him in on Mrs. Edgecombe's details about the mythology. Ahkai stares at me, then the tentacle, up at me again, and bites his lip.

He doesn't believe me.

"But all the evidence adds up," I say in a small voice. "It doesn't make sense, but it all adds up."

"The mind is powerful enough to manifest fears into reality," he replies. "Is there the slightest possibility that you are so scared for Uncle Vince to be in a relationship, that you imagined all these supernatural signs?"

Dejected, I flop down on the step.

Ahkai sits next to me. "Mums are cool, you know."

I think about earlier this morning, when Daddy gifted me with new memories of Mummy. He's never been able to speak about her before. What changed?

Mariss . . .

The day Mariss came into our lives, Daddy was able to talk about Mum and, for the first time, remove a bit of her presence from the closet. Since then, Mariss must have cured more than a bad knee; she's healing him from the inside. That's why it's easier for Daddy to talk about Mum; Mariss's devotion is easing his inner pain.

If only she were human . . .

"Oh, I nearly forgot," Ahkai says. He lifts his chain off and puts it around my neck.

"Tanjoubi omedetou!" he cries, and adds, "that's 'happy birthday' in Japanese."

My mouth drops open, and I hold the hummingbird in my hand. "Your lucky charm."

"*Your* lucky charm. Now I have this." He pulls out a similar chain, but he's whittled a sleeping cat.

"Simba?" I ask.

He nods and puts the new chain around his neck. He's accepted that Simba most likely is not coming back. Ahkai looks down at the wooden cat resting against his chest and smiles.

How? How did he get over this so quickly? I don't understand. I'm glad he's feeling better, but I just don't understand.

I get up and dust the dirt off my romper. "Let's go to the zoo."

We walk through a tunnel with cut rock, and then it opens into a large space surrounded by tall trees with hanging vines. There's a yellow sign with a green monkey: WELCOME TO BARBADOS WILDLIFE RESERVE.

Different kinds of birds roam about the space, and one bird is so friendly it comes right up to Ahkai and hops onto his shoe. All the visitors ignore the CAUTION: DO NOT FEED THE ANIMALS sign and throw bits of fruit and vegetables to them.

Pigeon poop drops right onto Daddy's forehead, and though I'm stressed out, I can't help but smile. Mariss manages to get a picture before he cleans it off. After that, I'm able to relax a little bit.

Ahkai has a way with animals; they all approach him

to be fed—the peacocks, turtles, and even parrots fly down from the tops of the trees. Mariss gives me the small digital camera, and I get a cool picture of him teaching the parrot how to say its true name, "psittacine."

Mariss, Daddy, and Ahkai walk ahead of me on the cobbled brick path through the forest. They're laughing and pointing at the rabbits and deer that peek out from the trees. I snap a picture of them to remember this moment, the moment I realized that having a new mum—one who wasn't Mariss—and maybe even a younger brother wouldn't be so bad.

The thought of a new family melts a wall around my heart, and I feel the urge to cry.

As if by fate, a baby green monkey swings down from a tree. It's so cute with its tiny black face, golden-green fur, and white belly. Ahkai stops to talk to the baby monkey, or as he calls it, the *Chlorocebus sabaeus.*

The curious monkey comes closer to him, and Mariss steps forward, holding out a piece of fruit. I lift the camera, anticipating another sentimental moment, but the baby monkey surprises us all when it jumps back and bares its teeth.

Daddy pulls Ahkai away and steps in front of him and

Mariss, shielding them from a potential attack. The baby monkey jumps up and down and screeches. It's transformed from a cuddly pet to an angry gremlin.

Three other monkeys, attracted by its cries, jump from the trees behind them, on the opposite side of the trail. I look for help, but there is no one else around. Daddy hasn't noticed the other monkeys, but Mariss looks over her shoulder. The monkeys all bare their teeth and prowl closer to her, hissing.

Mariss pulls off her shades and jerks her neck forward, as if she is planning to bite them.

I open my mouth to warn Daddy, and that's when I see it.

The side of Mariss's face changes to a muddy green, the color traveling up her face like it's a glass pitcher being filled with Kool-Aid. The bottom half of her face pops forward, like a piece of toast coming out of a toaster, and two curved fangs extend from her lips. She returns a hiss, much stronger than that of all the monkeys combined. It's similar to the sound Jalopy made one time when it was overheating. All the hairs on my arms stand on end. It's like I've been doused with a bucket of ice-cold water.

The monkeys retreat into the trees.

I am frozen. I beg my feet to move, my mouth to scream, but nothing happens. It's like I've turned into a tree; my feet are rooted to the spot. I remember the camera in my hand, and it takes all my willpower to squeeze down on the button.

Click.

I blink, and Mariss's face is back to normal. The baby monkey hurries away.

She stares at me, and I stare at her. The beat of my pulse races to my head and pounds in my ears.

I gawk as her yellow eyes fade to a lighter yellow, to milky white, and then back to dark brown. She puts on her sunglasses in a swift, smooth motion.

Daddy looks around at us. "Everybody all right?" he asks. He notices my frozen horror, but Mariss distracts him, throwing her body against his.

"My hero!" exclaims Mariss. I gag as he gives her a peck on the mouth.

No one is going to believe me.

They hold hands and continue down the path, but Ahkai's watching Mariss too . . . maybe he saw her transformation.

I yank him into the nearest brick building.

"D-D-Did you see?" I spit out the words, but he doesn't reply. He's too busy reading labels and descriptions.

"Tell me you saw!" I shout, trying to steady my trembling feet. I clutch the wall to stop myself from falling.

"Saw what?" he asks, and points at something behind me. I jump around, expecting to see Mariss's fangs bearing down on me, but instead, I find snakes curled up in glass cages.

We are in the snake house.

Ahkai shakes his finger at a cage with a light-green-and-brown snake hanging from a branch. He reaches into his pocket and pulls out the transparent tentacle.

"Interesting," he murmurs.

I spy what has captured his attention. At the bottom of the cage, transparent with a diamond pattern, just like the tentacle, is a large piece of snake skin.

"The bottom half of her body could be like a snake too," I whisper, remembering Mrs. Edgecombe's words. Keeping my back against the wall, I slide to the ground, my eyes glued to the entrance in case Mariss decides to come after me.

I knew she was a sea spirit, but I never expected it would be as horrible as this. I have to warn Daddy; I don't care if he breaks every plate in the house. I have to persuade him to listen to me this time.

That's when I remember the camera, still clenched in my hands. I have proof!

I turn on the camera to show Ahkai the evidence. Oh, how he will grovel when he realizes I've been right all along. And Daddy will be able to witness the ugly truth with his own two eyes.

I press the button, but the camera does not come on. The screen remains blank.

No no.

I pop open the compartment to fiddle with the battery, and green smoke sizzles out of the camera.

The batteries and memory card have all melted.

CHAPTER 18

Ahkai and I are quiet in the back seat, while Daddy and Mariss babble on about picnicking and the weather. Mariss is acting as if nothing happened, and it makes me even more anxious. Every time she puts an arm around Daddy, I imagine her wrapping around his body and squeezing the life out of him.

Ahkai is beyond skeptical. He claims the camera must have overheated but can't explain how snake skin could have ended up in Mr. Pimples's tank. The silver lining is that he's agreed to help me do research, or as he said, disprove the folklore. He's adamant that the snake skin could not have come from a mythical half-woman, half-snake creature.

As we approach the top of Coconut Hill, the silk cotton tree looms above us, and I flash back to a time when my biggest worry was my daddy having a regular, normal girlfriend. Fairy Vale Academy appears in the distance.

"Daddy! I forget to tell you!" How could this have slipped my mind? "Miss Alleyne wake up!"

"What!" Daddy slams on the brake and we all jolt forward. The loud screech scares the blackbirds from the branches, and they soar over the ocean.

"Vincey, we should get home." Mariss twists in her seat, glancing behind at the road. A strong wind rattles through the leaves, and she frantically rolls up her window, then pats her afro back into place.

I sneak glances at Mariss while telling him about the lionfish attack, careful not to say anything that may trigger her, but she's not paying any attention. She's lost in thought; there's actually a crease in her plastic forehead.

BEEEEEEP.

A truck horn blares behind us. Mariss jumps so high she would have crashed through Jalopy's roof if not for the seatbelt. Fearing an attack, I dive down in the back seat, nearly losing a tooth to Ahkai's knee.

Daddy peers into the rearview mirror and pulls to the

side so the truck can pass. "I'll visit her tomorrow." He puts Jalopy into gear and continues on.

"Excuse me, we have plans tomorrow." There is a chill in Mariss's voice.

Daddy glances over at Mariss and sighs. "We can go to the park another time, Sisi. This is Bean's teacher . . . and a friend."

"Just a friend?" Mariss still has on her shades, but I sense a change in the air. Are her eyes yellow? Will she attack now?

"'Ow much times I must tell you so, Sisi?"

I look at Ahkai, and as usual, he's ignoring the conflict.

"We come first—"

"Not in front of the children," Daddy interrupts her. She folds her arms across her chest and grinds her teeth. There's no more talking in the car afterward.

I shrink into the seat and chew on my fingernails, desperate for an excuse to stop him from visiting Miss Alleyne at the hospital. If Daddy ditches Mariss, it may push her over the edge. I'm so distracted that I don't realize we've parked and I'm alone in Jalopy, until Daddy calls from the kitchen.

That night, I sit in bed with a flashlight, staring at the

locked door, terrified that when the sun rises, Daddy will not.

I try to convince myself that he's safe. *Mariss loves him . . . She would never hurt him . . .*

I reach under the pillow for the folklore book, grateful that tonight should be my last time rereading the heavy text, looking for clues. Ahkai will speed-read the pages tomorrow and I might actually be able to get a few hours sleep.

The word "shape-shifter" gets my attention.

The Lagahoo looks like a normal creature during the day, but at night it takes the form of a man with a wooden coffin for a head. It carries heavy iron chains around its neck, one of which is tied like a noose around its waist and trails behind him.

I think about Casper and his wild ramblings about the Heartman kidnapping his wife. *Suppose he was telling the truth?* I feel so ashamed about the practical joke I pulled with the chain. It's clear that Fairy Vale is far from the ordinary, boring fishing village I believed it to be.

The wind howls, and my curtain flaps in the air. I vault out of bed and slam the window closed. This is worse than watching a horror movie before going to sleep. I'm way too traumatized to keep reading, but as I'm closing the book, my eyes land on a blue scrawl near the bottom of the page:

"Mater Maris?"

I sit upright when I read the paragraph under the heading "Sea Spirit."

> A SEA SPIRIT: A mermaid-like figure with a woman's upper body and the hindquarters of a fish or serpent. A large snake is usually wrapping itself around her body and laying its head between her breasts. She is known for her mysticism and her vengeance. Using her beautiful voice, she abducts the unfortunate or mean-spirited while they are swimming or boating, and drowns them at the bottom of the sea. But she could also bring good fortune; she carries expensive baubles and it is believed that anyone who finds her treasure will become rich. But be warned, a pact with a sea spirit often requires great sacrifice. If one accepts a sea spirit's invaluable gift, it is an invitation of her presence into their life. The only means of escape is to

I press a hand to my chest and take a deep breath, trying to calm my racing heartbeat. It's a lot to process. Documented facts about a sea spirit. A great sacrifice. Drowning.

I wipe beads of sweat from my nose, all of a sudden feeling suffocated, like the room is shrinking. Daddy is in so much danger. He's not safe on land but is even more vulnerable when he's out at sea. He's trapped, like in that terrible dream I had when all roads led to death. I can't help but imagine Mariss dragging him along the sea floor.

I push the morbid thought aside, struggling to keep my breath steady. No one is going to drown my daddy while I'm still alive. My finger shakes as I slide it across to next page, my skin tingling with anticipation. After being in the dark for so long, at last I'm on the verge of finding out how to get rid of Mariss. I brace myself for whatever's coming next, ready to do anything necessary to save my daddy.

But the line at the top of the page starts with a new sentence. I flick to the previous page, checking that none of them are stuck together, and that's when I notice the jagged tear inside the crease.

Someone has ripped out the page.

I fall back onto the bed, heaving and staring at the ceiling, trying not to scream with frustration. It's like I'm a cat, pawing at a dangling string that some sadistic human pulls away as soon as I'm within reach. To make matters worse, Mrs. Edgecombe said this book was the only copy in the library.

Mrs. Edgecombe! She may know what's on the missing page.

I stare at darkness until sunlight tickles the window, then I drag myself downstairs to get energy from some extra-strong ginger tea. I almost trip on the stairs and have to hold on to the railing to keep from falling.

Daddy and Mariss are at the table again, and I rush to hug Daddy. I avoid looking at Mariss and press my head on his chest to listen to his heartbeat. He makes a limp attempt to return my embrace, but then pats me away and opens a newspaper. I grab some cereal and then sit so close to him at the table that the edge of his newspaper gets soaked in my milk.

It's still tense.

I didn't think it was possible to miss the quiet tinkling of knives and forks. Mariss shoots daggers at Daddy from across the table, not bothering to hide her anger. If she remains this enraged, Daddy will be kissing the bottom of the ocean in no time. He's been staring down at the same newspaper article for the last ten minutes, like he's afraid to break the silence with the sound of a turning page.

I'm so sleep-deprived that I'm wondering if I dreamt up everything that happened yesterday. I close my eyes and pinch my hand, hoping I'll see Mariss with a green rubber mask in her hands, saying "Gotcha!"

I open my eyes and Mariss is staring right at me.

Her pupils flash yellow. I yelp and fall off the chair.

"Bean?" Daddy looks under the table at me. "What 'appen?"

"N-Nothing, nothing," I stutter, looking at Mariss. She smirks and sips her juice.

I head to the kitchen to scrape most of my cornmeal porridge into the trash, but then I notice pieces of burnt paper at the top of the waste bin. A piece of the paper crumbles in my hand, but its yellowed, splotched edges are an exact match to the pages in the folklore book.

Mariss must have snuck into my room and ripped out the page!

I rush upstairs to get ready for school, now even more desperate to talk to Mrs. Edgecombe.

Jalopy's been reinfected with its old cough, and to make matters worse, every pothole feels like a blow to my head. The backs of my eyes are burning, yet I'm scared to close them while Mariss is in the car. Daddy doesn't say a word about Miss Alleyne, and I don't dare bring her up. Not while Mariss is around.

Even Ahkai is unnerved by the silence. He hums a cheerful tune to fill the eerie void all the way to school.

Daddy parks next to Casper's empty guard hut. I haven't seen him, but I know he's still around because the area is free of garbage, with not even a pebble among the green grass.

"Mariss!" Coach Broomes comes up to Jalopy with his smiling grimace. "Always lovely to see you!" Then a frosty, "Vincent."

Coach hasn't forgiven Daddy for the volleyball loss. Daddy replies with a sharp nod.

"Good morning, Sean," Mariss chirps with fake enthusiasm. "You're looking very handsome this morning."

Instead of his regular Fairy Vale-branded polo shirt and track pants, Coach Broomes is wearing maroon-and-yellow West Indies cricket apparel.

"Thank you, little lady. We got a West Indies cricket scout here this morning, looking fuh promising cricketers for a training camp in St. Lucia next week, during term break."

A few months ago, the news of a West Indies cricket

scout at Fairy Vale would have been like a dream come true. Now I only dream of getting rid of Mariss. I need to get answers from Mrs. Edgecombe. I want my old life back.

But Mariss reaches through the window and grips my shoulder, preventing me from following Ahkai to the library. I hold my breath and look down at her manicured red nails against my uniform.

"You hear that, Josie? You have a chance to show off your skills in St. Lucia!"

Both Daddy and Coach Broomes protest at the same time.

"It's what Miss Alleyne would have wanted," Mariss retorts, all the sugar gone from her voice. "Isn't that right, Vincey?"

I don't look around, but I feel the shift in Mariss's body. Her palm starts to get hot on my shoulder.

"Yes," Daddy says, his voice slow and full of uncertainty. He has the dazed, blank expression. *Mariss is bewitching him!* "You are right. It is an excellent idea." Coach Broomes exhales through flared nostrils.

I jerk away from her grip. Mariss has never been enthusiastic about my cricket so it's obvious she only wants to send me away.

"Coach, I don't want—"

"Then it's settled!" Mariss cuts me off and gets out of Jalopy. "And I'll stay to give Josie some moral support." She hooks her arm through Coach Broomes's and urges him through the gate. Daddy presses on the gas and peels off, not even telling me goodbye.

There's no way I can leave for a cricket camp now. Who knows what Mariss will do to Daddy while I'm gone?

I'm going to have to throw my game. The thought leaves a horrible taste in my mouth but I have no choice.

Ahkai is waiting for me inside the gate. I step in front of him, pull the folklore book from my backpack, and open it to the missing page. He immediately notices the vandalism.

"Who damaged this antique?" Ahkai looks up at me, his eyes filled with accusation.

"I swear it wasn't me." I gesture at Mariss, who is a few feet ahead, laughing in Coach Broomes's face. I reach into my pocket and show Ahkai a piece of the burnt page.

"She *is* a monster!" exclaims Ahkai. "A desecrater of literature!"

I take advantage of Ahkai's outrage. "Go to Mrs. Edgecombe and find out what was on that page," I urge. Mariss is giving me a dark look, all while flirting with

Coach Broomes. "Mariss is trying to destroy invaluable knowledge."

Ahkai salutes, hides the book behind his bag, and speed-marches toward the library.

This time, instead of watching from the stands, Mariss sits on a bench next to the tamarind tree, avoiding the shade from its bright green leaves. Her amber highlights shimmer in the sun, which is already fiery hot even though it's only after nine in the morning.

Coach Broomes introduces the representative from the West Indies cricket board—a large, bored-looking man who examines us while picking his teeth with his fingernail. I don't have my games clothes and I stick out like a bubblegum stain on a white wall in my horrid blue-and-pink uniform. I can't even be mad at the snickering behind me when I walk out onto the field in my long pleated skirt and a helmet.

My starched cotton blouse clings to my body, soaked in sweat, but I try to ignore my discomfort. I make four feeble attempts to hit the ball, making sure to miss every time.

The bowler sprints toward me, sweat flying off his arms as he does his run-up. I prepare to miss the ball again, but then there's a tingling sensation on my arm.

Huh? I peer down and see beads of salty sweat trembling like Jell-O and moving down to my fingers like a parade of dancing spiders.

Before I can process the bizarre experience, the bowler releases the ball. I move my bat away, but the ball swerves and collides with my bat so hard my teeth rattle.

CRACK!

The ball sails over the boundary, out toward the tamarind tree. Coach Broomes drops his clipboard in shock.

"Six runs!" The West Indies rep breaks the stunned silence with loud applause.

It's like the ball had a mind of its own. There's no way I could have hit it that far. The ball disappears into the thick branches and then falls into Mariss's waiting palms.

She gives me a slow smile before tossing the ball onto the field.

This has to be her doing, but how is she controlling cricket balls? She's a saltwater spirit, and unlike the waves and fish, balls are not related to the sea in any way.

Another bead of sweat rolls down my ear, and the droplet shivers, tickling my earlobe, and then makes a sharp U-turn into my earhole. I slap the side of my head, and just like that, I understand.

Sweat.

She's using sweat to manipulate the ball.

It makes sense because it's just another form of salt water. She can guide the ball in any direction, once there's enough sweat on its surface. And Mariss has more than enough supply from this drenched bowler.

The bowler runs up again and bowls the ball. I dig my heels into the ground, determined not to move, but the ball crashes into my bat again without my help, going over the school walls, so far past the boundary it could be counted as twelve runs.

"Cheese on bread!" The West Indies rep is beside himself, beaming and scribbling in his notepad.

When it's my turn to bowl, Mariss may use my sweat to direct the ball into the stumps. If I don't do something fast, I'll be on my way to St. Lucia and leaving Daddy to her mercy.

I stomp off the cricket field and fling my helmet onto the floor in the girls' changing room. How am I supposed to fight Mariss when the sun and my own body heat are on her side?

"Think think think think think," I repeat, rocking on a bench and clutching my head. How do I stop sweating? I'm sure there is some scientific way to block the pores. I think about Mr. Atkins's science classes and wish I had paid more attention to the notes on the blackboard.

And that's when a solution hits me.

I sneak into Coach Broomes's equipment room. *This has to work . . .* I can't leave Daddy alone with Mariss.

When it's my turn to bowl, I walk to the end of the pitch, my pockets heavy. I can already feel the tickling around the back of my neck and along my arms as Mariss works her sea powers, but this time I'm prepared.

I swirl my right hand around in my pocket. When I pull it out, it's as white as a blank page, covered in powdered chalk, courtesy of the gymnastics students. I've seen them dusting their hands with the powder to help absorb sweat and also to get a better grip on the bars. I pat the powder on the ball and along my arms. Now most of my skin is as dry as ash.

Mariss gets up from the bench. She's not smirking anymore.

Every bad ball I bowl chips away at a piece of my soul, and my ego gets smaller and smaller, until I feel as worthless as the mud underneath my sneakers. There's no way I'll be chosen for the camp now.

Both Jared and Coach Broomes are looking at me

with suspicion, so for my last ball I bowl as fast as I can, but I make sure it is off target. The batsman swings and misses, the pace too quick for him, and the ball goes wide of the stumps and rolls down to the boundary.

Everyone probably thinks I am chasing after the ball, but I run past the boundary and to the closest place of isolation I can think of—the toolshed at the back of the school.

I collapse at the edge of the small swamp and hide my face in my knees. I sniffle, thinking about the disappointment in Jared's eyes, and water slides out of my nose. I welcome the mosquito bites as some form of punishment.

I'm feeling so sorry for myself that at first, I ignore the small splashes. But when I raise my head there are hundreds, maybe even thousands, of tiny brown fish popping out of the water. They move toward me like a swarm of bees drawn to an island of honey. Like they want to engulf my body and feed on my skin.

I gasp and scramble away from the edge, unable to take my eyes off the fish. I didn't even know that fish lived in the swamp—the most I'd seen were frogs and tadpoles. The small fish reach the edge of the water, and to my surprise, they fling themselves into the mud, beaching themselves like whales, desperate to reach me. No normal fish would behave like this, but then I think about the flying lionfish in the Hot Pot.

This has to be another warning from Mariss. I need to find out how to stop her.

I take one last look at the fish in the grass, their tiny mouths gasping for air, and dash toward the library.

CHAPTER 19

I race through the corridors, trying my best to avoid colliding with other students strolling down the halls like they're taking a walk on the beach. It's hard to process that they're still children leading normal lives, only stressing about homework because they've never been attacked by gasping zombie fish.

I slide to a stop before reaching the end of the building; there's an exposed space ahead. I've crossed the path countless times to get to the library, but never once realized I'd be in full view of the pasture. Until now.

If Mariss is still on the cricket field, I'll be in her line of sight.

I peek around the corner and recognize the back of

Coach Broomes, but from that angle I can't see if Mariss is on the bench. I lean forward as much as I can, then nearly fall flat on my face when someone bangs on the piano in the music room.

Just go for it, I urge myself. I draw deep breaths and then sprint toward the library. I can't help but look over my shoulder, and I get relief at the sight of the empty bench before disappearing inside.

Mrs. Edgecombe is at the counter with the folklore book open in front of her, and there's no sign of Ahkai. She shoots me an annoyed look when I rush up to her.

"Josephine, I told you to take care of this book!"

"Ma'am, I swear it wasn't me." I catch my breath and cross my heart to prove I'm not lying. "I'll explain later, but I need to know what was on that page."

Mrs. Edgecombe removes her glasses and leans over the counter. "Well, I do happen to have—"

"Josie Sweets." Mrs. Edgecombe pauses at the sound of Mariss's sultry voice behind me. I grip on to the counter, and would have leapt over it to escape if Mrs. Edgecombe weren't blocking me.

Mariss glides toward us in her white wrap dress, looking like an angel to all unsuspecting victims. Her smile does not reach her eyes.

"I just wanted to see if you were okay, after your . . .

performance." She rests a hot hand on my shoulder and I make a strangled sound.

Mariss extends the hand to Mrs. Edgecombe. "Greetings, sister."

Mrs. Edgecombe shakes Mariss's hand, but oddly enough, doesn't let go. Mariss looks down at the folklore book, and then into Mrs. Edgecombe's eyes, giving her famous wide smile.

"I love books, but be careful," Mariss says, resting her other hand on Mrs. Edgecombe's curved back. "Reading can be dangerous."

Mrs. Edgecombe's hunched back straightens like curly hair with a hot comb. They finally break their handshake, and Mrs. Edgecombe lowers her head, as if bowed in prayer.

All this time I am tense, afraid to breathe, now that Mariss is making threats in broad daylight. Thank goodness there are no fish in the library.

"Well, I'm off. Sorry I can't spend more time with you, Josie, but you know what they say." Mariss softens her voice. "There's no rest for the wicked."

I can't help but touch the dark circles under my eyes.

"Goodbyeee," Mariss sings in a fake sad voice.

Mrs. Edgecombe and I stare after her as she floats to the exit, and as soon as she's out of sight, we both exhale.

"Listen to me, Josephine." Mrs. Edgecombe is flustered, her voice raspy. "If you upset someone like that, you gotta make amends. You hear me?"

"But, ma'am, what if it's too late?" I whisper, pleading with my eyes. "What was on that page?"

Mrs. Edgecombe looks at the exit, then down at me, all sorts of emotions flashing across her face. Fear. Pity. Sadness. Fear again.

"I don't know what to tell you," Mrs. Edgecombe replies in an extra-loud voice, as if we're being watched.

She grips the folklore book and hurries away, her back straighter than a cricket stump.

"Please, ma'am, please help me." I follow her until she locks herself in the bathroom. But I continue to bang at the door, until there are annoyed cries from other students.

I press my forehead against the door. "Ma'am, I can't lose my daddy too."

A few seconds later, a piece of paper slides out from under the door. I grab it and hurry to a secluded area in the library. After checking to make sure I'm not being followed, I unfold the paper.

It's a printout of the missing page! Mrs. Edgecombe must have preserved a digital scan of the book for her records. I feel a rush of gratitude for the librarian as I devour the words:

> The only means of escape is to revoke the invitation into one's life by returning the gift to her underwater kingdom, a journey that is certain death unless taken at a time when a sea spirit is most vulnerable. Until then, she has the power to maintain control of one's mind through fantastic dreams and entice one to her, and they will follow her to their death at the bottom of the sea. It is best not to make trouble with a sea spirit because the captive's release often hinges on some sort of priceless demand, ranging from total devotion to the spirit to the death of a loved one.

I slide down to the floor, still staring at the page. The paper shakes in my hand as I focus on the words "certain death." A repressed memory rises up and pulls my mind underwater; I'm drowning and reaching into empty darkness, this time not for a silver dollar but for my daddy.

I will have to go somewhere deep in the ocean, but

before I make that journey, I have to relinquish Mariss's control over Daddy.

I have to find the gift.

I swallow my fear and rack my brain, trying to remember Mariss's gifts. My guess would have been the necklace with the spiral pendant, but I threw that into the sea and she's still here. Maybe I didn't throw it in the right spot?

Unlike the original book, there's no scrawled handwriting in the margins. The book must have been scanned before the annotations. I don't know what Mariss's gift is. I don't know the exact location of her underwater lair. I don't know *when* to go—"most vulnerable" isn't a time on my watch.

I feel so hopeless . . . and there's no one to help me.

Then, I spot Ahkai, rushing toward me like a brave hero coming to save the day. I expect good news, judging from the eager look on his face. When he gets close, he waves the burnt piece of paper in front of me.

"I used glycerin in the science lab to restore ink from the burnt page," Ahkai says in an excited manner.

The words "full moon" are clear in the blue scribble on the charred page. The scrawl lifts the fog of confusion in my brain.

Is Mariss most vulnerable at the full moon? Last full

moon Mariss *was* outside after dark; I get chills when I remember Daddy's trance-like state. And the full moon before that—wait, Mariss wasn't even around. It's hard to believe so little time has passed since she began wreaking havoc on my life. Nothing special happened on that full moon—

I gasp as I recall the image of the jeweled brass comb in the moonlight. That's the night Daddy had his nightmare . . . about fangs. I remember the magical way that comb glided through my curls.

That's the gift. I have to return the comb during a full moon! BUT where? I glance over at Ahkai. He's already lost interest in the burnt paper and is deep in a book about marine life. He's not going to indulge me right now.

Still, a tiny spark of hope ignites in my chest. I have a lot of unanswered questions, but at long last, I have a path to getting rid of Mariss, and the first step is simple.

Find the comb.

And Daddy should know where it is.

I'm glad when I see Jalopy parked outside the house that afternoon. Daddy's at the table again, shifting through bills and tapping on the calculator. I've never seen him look so old—even the gray hairs have spread along the sides of his head. It's like Mariss is draining the life out of him.

"Daddy, I want you to redo my hair," I say, pretending to undo one of the plaits. "Where's that comb you had? The one you found in the net."

He doesn't look up from the bills. "What comb?"

"The brass one, with the jewels," I reply with a hint of frustration.

Daddy scoffs. "If I 'ad a comb with jewels it would solve all my problems."

"But—"

He waves a hand to silence me, muttering numbers under his breath. For a second, I want to throw the calculator out the window, but then decide it's better to first search the last place I saw the comb: his bedroom.

The inside of Daddy's room has transformed. It's like a page out of a lifestyle magazine. There are several red and white pillows on his bed, and light blue curtains by the window sparkle like the sunlight on the ocean. A strong lavender scent engulfs the room.

I try the closet first and I'm immediately drawn to a large, unfamiliar cardboard box on the lower shelf. I pull at the masking tape and rip open the flap.

"Josephine."

I jump back, slamming against the closet door, and turn around slowly.

Mariss is in the doorway, her eyes bright with anger. My blood goes cold.

"Those are my belongings." She takes one step inside, her eyes boring into mine. "What are you searching for?"

I move toward the doorway, my back pressed against the wall. All excuses die on my lips as we stare at each other, and my throat tightens, closing up like I'm deathly allergic to being caught red-handed.

Maybe this is the moment she'll attack, now that she knows I know the truth about her identity. Can she look in my eyes and see that I know how to get rid of her? That I know once the comb is returned, she'll lose all control over Daddy? Maybe she'll claw my face apart while he's downstairs doing math.

I jump as Mariss makes another move, but she goes over to the bed and sits on the crisp sheets. She breaks our eye contact, her gaze shifting to the closet. She stares at it and traces spirals with her fingernail across one of the white pillows.

I take a chance and dash to the door, expecting fangs to sink into my back, but nothing happens. I slam my bedroom door behind me, then buckle against it as I glance at the calendar.

The next full moon is tomorrow.

CHAPTER 20

My eyes fly open at the same time the brass clock strikes three.

It's been eight minutes since my last nightmare; seems like sleepless nights are part of my routine now. In the last bad dream, Daddy forced me through the departure gate at the airport, and when I turned to wave goodbye, the back of his head twisted into Mariss's smiling face.

"Enjoy cricket camp!" Daddy-Mariss sang. Their arm flipped around like an OPEN & CLOSED hanging sign to return my wave.

From the window, the almost-full moon is bright and shimmering in the sky. Once before, its light brought me peace; now it's like an eerie danger sign.

Just when I'm tempted to close my eyes again, a

shadow covers the bottom of the door, blocking out the light from the hallway. I pinch myself to make sure it's not another nightmare.

The doorknob turns, until *click*, the lock prevents it from going any farther.

Whew.

Then *BANG*! The doorknob swings all the way around. I scream at the top of my lungs.

"Bean?" Daddy yells. Now light appears from the hallway again, and Daddy rushes into my room.

"Bean, don't worry, is just a bad dream," he says, limping over to the bed. He groans when he sits down, and I bury my face in his chest.

"Don't leave me, please," I cry out.

"I'm 'ere. I ain' going nowhere." He holds me until my wheezing slows back down to normal breathing.

"Lookie here, I'm the parent again," he jokes, and I can't help but smile. "What you dream that 'ad you so frighten?" he asks.

I tell him the truth. "That you left me."

"Oh, Bean, you know that won't ever 'appen."

"Can you stay until I go back to sleep?" I ask. It is a trick. Whenever he stays, Daddy always ends up falling asleep with me. Right now, I don't want him out of my sight.

"To tell you the truth, I dunno if I can get up," Daddy says, slapping his knee. "I think Mariss threw out the Benjie's . . ." His voice trails off.

"Wait a minute!" I look under the bed and pull out a tube of Benjie's. It rolled under there ages ago, but I was too lazy to get it.

I rub a generous amount of the vapor rub onto his bad knee. He lets out a long "ahhhh."

"You have to remember you're not young, Daddy." I rub his knee clockwise, then anti-clockwise.

"'Ush your mouth and rub the next knee," Daddy replies. "It's been acting up lately. Maybe I should see a doctor."

"For old age?" I ask cheekily, putting the balm on the other knee. But even as I joke, I'm worried because this knee has never given Daddy any problems. At that moment, I also notice there are gray hairs at the top of his head.

Daddy sucks his teeth. "I don't know where you get all that mouth from."

"I get it from you!"

Daddy laughs, and then ruffles my hair. "I miss this, yuh know."

A time before Mariss.

It's like Daddy reads my mind. "I'll ask Mariss 'ow much longer till 'er roof is finished."

"Wait—no!" I exclaim, and Daddy arches his eyebrow. I want Mariss out of the house, yes, but she commanded a mutant lionfish to attack Miss Alleyne and sent zombie fish after me when I upset her. With just a look, she reduced the normally boisterous Mrs. Edgecombe to a nervous cockroach hiding in the bathroom. If Daddy asked her to leave she'd lure him to the bottom of the sea for sure. And he would follow her to his death, willingly turn himself into fish food under her control.

"Somebody finally warming up to Mariss?" Daddy asks in a teasing voice.

"Uh, no, it's just that, uh." I search my brain for a lie. "She told me it should be done in about two weeks, and she, uh, feels really sad that she has to leave, so best not to bring it up. Don't say anything."

"Mmm." Daddy settles into my pillow.

"How's Miss Alleyne?" I ask, remembering his plan to visit the hospital today.

"I ain' bother go, man," he replies, yawning. "We can all visit this weekend." I breathe a sigh of relief at one less problem to worry about, thankful that Daddy recognized the need to keep the peace. After a few minutes, he starts to snore, and I ease off the bed to close the door. The doorknob jiggles when I push it, and even in the dim light, I can tell it's broken. There's no way to keep Mariss out if she comes after me again.

I get back under the sheets and stare at the door until the roosters crow, their loud cries now sounding like strangled warnings. Daddy and I can't survive living with Mariss for much longer. We're both already on her bad side; I'm so tired I can barely see straight, and I've never seen Daddy more frail. I don't think he has the strength to fight against Mariss's mind control, even if he wanted to. It's up to me to free him from her spell.

I have to find that comb and return it to her lair today.

"Knock knock!" chirps Mariss, pushing open the door with her pinkie. I glare at her, my eyes red from lack of sleep, and squeeze Daddy a bit tighter.

She smirks at us cuddled together in the bed. "I didn't get an invite to the sleepover." I can't help but cower under the sheet as she steps inside my room. She's wearing a bigger spiral pendant today.

"I'm up! I'm up!" says Daddy. He untangles himself from my sheet.

Mariss takes a step back and wrinkles her nose. "What's that smell?"

"Oh, just a lil Benjie's Balm for my knee," Daddy replies. Without thinking, I roll over on top of the tube before she can confiscate it.

"Those chemicals can kill you. Please get rid of it," states Mariss, as if talking to a child. "I'll make some turmeric tea to help with the pain."

Mariss hurries away. Daddy and I exchange a look.

"Well, I better get ready." Daddy stands and stretches. "I ain' catch a thing yesterday, so me and some fellas going up north to see 'ow the fish biting. I will be 'ome late."

"How late?" I demand, trying to hide the anxiety in my voice. "Maybe you should give the fish a break and try again next week." Hopefully by then it will be safe for him to go out to sea.

"Bean, relax," he says. "One evening with Mariss ain' gine kill you." His ominous words hang in the air.

"Your tea is ready, Vincey!" Mariss calls from downstairs. Daddy makes a face.

"Don't worry, Daddy. Later we can make soup, and you can have all the dumplings you want."

He smiles and pinches my cheek, and I watch him hobble out of the room, wishing I could lock him away in a safe place.

I check the doorknob. It's broken all right, almost

falling off the door. Mariss tried to come in last night; now I'm even more determined to find the comb before she gets another chance.

I press my ear against my bedroom door and hear Daddy and Mariss bickering downstairs, so I scurry across the hall to Daddy's bedroom to search that box in the closet.

But the door is locked.

I resist the urge to pound my fist on the door, and exhale, trying to clear my mind. Mariss wouldn't have locked the door if there was nothing hidden inside. I'm sure the comb is in that box, and I'm not going to let something as simple as a locked door keep me out, not when a master lock picker lives right next door.

Ahkai is talented with a whittling knife, but I found out the extent of his skill when he used it to break into Mr. Atkins's drawer after he confiscated my cricket ball and one of Ahkai's favorite books.

I just have to persuade him to help me.

I get ready for school as normal. I have to stick to the same routine so Mariss doesn't suspect anything. If I faked a sickness, she would probably volunteer to stay home with me. But I plan to skip school with Ahkai and break into Daddy's bedroom.

Now that my home is enemy territory, after I'm dressed,

I peer out into the hallway for any sign of Mariss. She's in the shower, this time belting a sharp, fast-paced opera tune instead of her hocus-pocus wedding hymn. I confirm that Daddy's bedroom door is still locked before hurrying past the bathroom and through the steam floating out from under the door. She's draining all the hot water from the pipes.

Daddy's downstairs by the bar, scowling and scooping vegetable gunk off the counter and into a bowl. "Pass some tissue there, Jo."

Eager for him to leave, I search the cupboard for paper towels but find bags of table salt, sea salt, brown rice, and basmati rice on the top shelf. I remember Miss Mo talking about the soucouyant, her hands bent like claws. "If yuh can't find she skin, put some grains of salt or rice around the house. She has to count them before she can come in and kill you!"

This theory is just as wacky as walking home backward with one shoe, but I haven't secured the comb yet, and it can't hurt to see if Mariss has other weaknesses. Mariss's cooking is so bland that perhaps salt really is her natural enemy.

I grab a large bag of salt, and sprinkle a line along the entrance to the kitchen. It looks like a white ants' trail.

"Don't worry about it, I gotta go." Daddy pushes the

bowl aside. "Ask Miss Mo to take you school or you can walk there with Mariss." Before I can utter a word, Daddy is out the door.

This is perfect. I know the comb is in Daddy's bedroom, but I still have no idea where Mariss's lair is located. Today I can tail her, and maybe she'll lead me straight to her watery kingdom.

The bathroom door creaks open, and I dash outside, not even pausing to put down the bag of salt. Then, I hide in the hibiscus bushes, peeking through the kitchen window, eager to see if the salt will be effective.

Finally, she appears, looking like a stony queen in a silky wrap dress with red-and-silver lines. It's so long that the bottom drags on the floor. All that's missing is a tiara.

Mariss pauses by the entrance, looking down at the trail of salt. I brace myself, preparing for whatever happens next.

Without further reaction, Mariss glides over the trail. Her dress doesn't even shift the grains.

I guess I can cross "salt" off the list. A gentle breeze rattles the leaves and Mariss turns toward the window. I duck, folding in my lanky frame as much as possible, until I remember that blue-and-pink plaid is the worst kind of camouflage. I scramble out of the bushes and sprint over to Miss Mo's house.

It's unusually quiet, and I find Ahkai in the kitchen, poring over a stack of books.

"Where's Miss Mo?" I ask, leaning back against the door.

"She left home at a much earlier time to carry out stocktaking at the market," he replies. Excellent, one less obstacle to face. Finally, the tide is turning in my favor.

Ahkai glances at me. "Why are you holding a bag of salt?" I reluctantly confess to the trap I staged for Mariss.

Ahkai stares at me without blinking. "It seems highly improbable that sodium chloride would prevent an attack from such a powerful creature, if it existed."

I ignore him and check to see if Mariss followed me. I wonder if her snake eyes can see through the crack in the curtains.

"Did you leave a banana peel for her to slip on? That would expose her calf's foot."

"A Sea Mumma doesn't have a calf's foot!" I shriek, throwing my hands in the air. *Is this how Miss Mo feels?* "You know she has to be half snake. We found the snake skin!"

He frowns. It's the one thing he can't explain. "It states here that the sea snake *does* shed its skin every four weeks on average. They rub against coral or other hard substances to loosen it."

I'm hit by the image of Mariss constantly rubbing her skin on the walls.

"Every four weeks?" I whisper.

"Yes, and the new epidermis is very delicate and easily damaged."

Now it makes sense. A full moon occurs once a month, so maybe that's why Mariss snuck out that night—to shed her, ew gross, skin. It's probably when she's at her most exposed, her most vulnerable. This is why I have to return the comb during the full moon! It's my best chance of success.

"Alpha Mike," I say in a solemn voice, and close the book. "We have a new mission."

I'm no Lagahoo so I change my appearance the old-fashioned way. I raid Miss Mo's closet and grab a long flowered skirt and a black-and-white cotton blouse. I check out my new look in the mirror.

Not bad.

I pull on a black, straight-haired wig hanging from the side of the chest of drawers and secure it in place with a wide-brimmed straw hat, then hunch my shoulders forward and take a few stiff steps. There's no way Mariss will recognize me in my old lady disguise.

I take a tan wicker purse with pearly white buttons

from a nail in the wall, and when I check inside, I find a few pieces of tissue paper and a couple of black-eyed peas at the bottom. No, a pack of peas didn't happen to burst in her bag; Miss Mo believes that black-eyed peas can ward off evil spirits. I grab a few of the peas and put them in Ahkai's pants pocket, ignoring his mocking expression.

I'm not taking any chances.

While Ahkai finds a disguise, I peek through the windows, making sure that we don't miss Mariss. It seems like the soul has been sucked from my house, like its bright burgundy walls have retreated to a murky brown.

I rush Ahkai to choose between three shirts, so he decides to wear all of them, finishing off his bulky outfit with a baseball cap and sunglasses. There are already beads of sweat on his forehead.

Ahkai looks through the binoculars.

"The target is approaching," he says into the walkie-talkie, even though I'm right next to him.

Tailing is not as simple as people think. It's hard to stay undetected, because the brain alerts you that something is out of the ordinary, or as Miss Mo would say, "a mind tell me." That's why Ahkai and I have to work together, ducking behind the coconut trees, trusting ourselves to let Mariss get out of sight, and taking short-cuts to regain a visual. Ahkai hides behind newspapers at bus stops and whispers into the walkie-talkie, updating me with Mariss's position.

Mariss looks straight ahead, even when other bystanders—the men in particular—wave at her or bid her greetings. A man sitting at the side of the road with a three-tooth smile chokes on his catcall. I don't know what Mariss did but he's abandoned his cement block by the time we pass by.

Mariss doesn't ever move her black case from her left hand to her right because it is getting heavy, and she doesn't look back once, which is why I can't understand how she gives me the slip as soon as I reach the bottom of Coconut Hill.

I stomp my foot into the ground and then turn left, assuming she's gone on to the fish market. But today, the market is unnervingly quiet, not bustling with its usual activity. Most of the stalls are empty, and the few stalls that are open have no fish displays, just vendors packing fish into freezers.

"I've lost the target. Do you have a visual? Over." Someone taps me on the shoulder, and I pull the hat low over my face before turning around.

It's Ahkai.

"Where is she?" I hiss. I can't afford to lose track of her; lives depend on it.

Ahkai raises his shoulder and sticks his palms out. Then he gasps and pushes me into a narrow space between two stalls. The wall is covered with peeling newspapers and sticky black grime.

"What—"

"Shhh!!!" Ahkai points to a figure.

It's Miss Mo!

I press my back farther onto the icky wall. Miss Mo stops at the stall in front of us. She just has to turn a little to her right and look down, and we'll be discovered. I'm already thinking about excuses as to why we aren't at school and why I'm dressed in her good church clothes.

"Valerie." Miss Mo talks to someone out of our view. "Do a storm special. Tuna, eight dollars a pound. I gine finish pack."

Storm?

I look at the sky. The clouds are gray, with the sun struggling to break through. I had confused the stillness of the impending storm with my nerves.

"Ramona!" Miss Mo cries out. "Looka you! Oh, thank the Lord for his mercies and blessings upon us!"

Ramona is out of sight as well. "It's a miracle, Auntie," she says.

I want to know what they're talking about. I inch toward the edge of the wall. Ahkai, who is trembling, holds on to my hand and shakes his head. I ignore him and crouch in the space, closer to the ground, which is filled with old newspaper and plastic bottles. Ahkai slides down next to me, muttering under his breath.

I take a peek.

Miss Mo is touching Ramona's belly. The small bump is clear from my angle. My mouth falls open, and I move back into the hiding place.

"Ramona's pregnant!" I whisper to Ahkai. He goes to put his hand to his mouth, but stops short on seeing the grime on his fingers. I know he remembers what I told him about the Sea Mumma. *She can even cure infertility.*

Maybe he's starting to believe me . . .

"Take all the fish you want, Mummy! Yuh eating for two now!" We hear the rustling of newspapers and plastic bags.

"Now, you should put castor oil on that belly now and rub down the pain. Heat it up first, and massage it in every day. I barely feel a thing when Ahkai pop out."

Ahkai looks mortified.

"Thanks, Auntie, I heading home before the rain come down." We catch a glimpse of Ramona's face when she turns to wave goodbye. I've never seen her eyes brighter. She is glowing.

"Look, the red flags up and fishermen securing the boats," says Valerie, the thick woman with braids who Miss Mo was talking to before.

This means Daddy will be home soon . . . and Mariss. I need to get home and find that comb.

Ahkai and I stop breathing when Miss Mo seems to look in our direction, out toward the shore.

"That foolish one Seifert ain' tying it properly! Seifert!" Miss Mo yells, heading down the path to the beach.

Now's our chance!

Ahkai and I ease out of the space. We move to go in the opposite direction, but then I pause.

"Excuse me, young girl," I say in a shaky, high-pitched voice. It's my best old woman imitation. Valerie turns to me.

"Better get home, hear?" she says, lifting a piece of plywood on a small window. "Government order a complete shutdown. Nobody ain' supposed to be outside after one."

"I looking for Mariss. She 'bout here?" I ask.

"Who?"

"Mariss. She got a big afro, sells jewelry here at the market?"

Valerie shakes her head. "Only one person selling jewelry, and that's a Rasta man. Never hear bout nobody name Mariss. What sorta name is that?"

There is a loud crack of thunder, and then the rain starts to drizzle.

CHAPTER 21

Ahkai is way past frustrated and miserable. We haven't eaten anything all day, and we both get soaked on our way back, but my fear is way greater than hunger. I don't care about my wet clothes, although Miss Mo forever warns me that having wet hair and clothes is the path to certain death.

Ahkai takes off his baseball cap when we turn onto our street.

"Ahkai?" He doesn't look around and walks a little faster.

"Please help me get into Daddy's room."

He picks up the pace.

"If we don't find the comb, I swear I'll stop. Please, Ahkai!"

I drop my shoulders when he turns left to go to his house, but he pauses, then looks back at me. "Let me get my whittling knife."

I follow him inside to gather as many weapons as I can in case Mariss shows up. I grab everything she dislikes: toilet cleaner, mosquito repellent. I even take unhealthy things like margarine and leftover fried chicken from the fridge.

"Your mind has cracked," declares Ahkai after seeing the items in my hands. I check the street for Mariss before hurrying up the pathway to my house.

"I know she's hiding the comb in that closet," I argue, following him to Daddy's room. "Why else would she have the bedroom door locked when she's just in the bath?"

Ahkai examines the doorknob and then shakes it.

"Tell me there isn't something fishy about that!" I insist.

He turns the knob, and *click*. The door opens. The next sentence dies on my tongue, and Ahkai gives me his blank, unblinking stare. If the door's unlocked, that means . . .

I rush to the closet, worried that the cardboard box is gone, but thankfully it's still there. I poke the box with the bottle of toilet cleaner, and then, using the spray nozzle, I lift the flap.

Just clothes.

I glance up at the clothing on the hangers; they're mainly Daddy's jeans and shirts, next to dresses—they're all long-sleeved and white, red, or a combination of both colors. *Mariss's outfits* . . .

I examine the colorful array of designs in the box. These aren't just any old clothes; these are Mum's clothes, all packed away in this box with the words "For Salvation Army" scrawled at the side in Daddy's handwriting.

It's like I've been punched in the gut.

I caress the soft materials. All the colors are still bright even though they've been shut away for five years. I lift a flower-print silk handkerchief to my nose.

Her scent is long gone, and all that remains is the musk of expired mothballs with a hint of mildew. These outfits deserve better; they belong on a vibrant, breathing person who can show off their beauty at parties and fashion events.

How things change . . .

A few months ago, I would have been horrified at the thought of giving Mum's clothes away.

When I close the box, I'm immediately overcome with a sense of loss, and I get a flash of Ahkai looking down at the whittled Simba pendant and smiling. I uncover the box and take out the silk handkerchief, then gently fold and push it into my jeans pocket.

I finally understand, and I feel much better.

Now she's always with me...

I push the box back into the darkness and open another drawer. Nothing here either except cotton balls and coins. I close the drawer, but notice it doesn't go all the way in. I open it again and push my fingers to the back, feeling between the crack.

"Aha!" I shout, pulling out the brass comb. *I* knew *it was real.*

"Tell me you don't see this!" I exclaim, waving the comb in Ahkai's face. He has no reaction, and for a second I wonder if the relic is invisible to males. Ahkai reaches for the comb, examines it, and then rolls his eyes.

He tosses the comb on the bed and walks toward the door.

"Wait a minute." I pick up the comb and study the markings. It seems to be the same spiral pattern that's on Mariss's pendant, but there is corrosion that prevents me from seeing the design.

REMOVES RUST AND MOLD is in bold purple letters on the label of the toilet cleaner, so I shake the bottle and spray the liquid on the comb. The corrosion clears away without me having to wipe it, and the spiral design is now as clear as day.

"Daddy told me he caught this comb in his net. Look, Ahkai!" I show him the marking. "This is the same spiral pendant Mariss wears."

"Interesting," he says, moving to examine the comb. "The symbol *does* look like a coiled serpent."

I am too relieved to gloat and yell "I told you so!" Instead, I wait on his logical brain to accept that between the snake skin, the animal disappearances, the folklore book, and now the comb, I've been right all along.

Then, the comb starts to heat up, and it gets heavier and heavier, so heavy I'm forced to cup it with both hands. Something weird is happening. It's like the comb is turning into a shot put ball and the spiral is getting darker and darker.

"Maybe the sulfuric acid in the cleaner is reacting to the metal," Ahkai says, scratching his chin. I drop the comb on the floor to keep it from burning my fingers and it lands on the carpet with an odd thud.

I chew on my lip as yellow splotches appear on the spiral. We should move away in case the acid causes the comb to explode in our faces. But my words of warning are lost when the spiral bursts into different shades of yellow that dance around like sunlight on bubbles. It's so captivating that I lean in closer, and a musty smell fills my nostrils, like decaying seaweed on a beach.

I lift a finger to poke the brass, and then . . . the spiral starts to wriggle.

And a black-and-gold snake pops out of the comb.

I jump back, just in time for its fangs to miss my face. I release a high-pitched scream, and Ahkai and I scatter in opposite directions.

The snake is about half an inch wide—the same width as an adult centipede, but it's faster. And deadlier. I can't just kill it with a shoe. It's as long as a ruler, maybe even longer since it's coiled against the bed. And it is *angry*.

Its yellow, deadpan eyes lock onto mine. I can't look away. I can't even blink.

The snake raises its head in the air, bringing itself to full height, and draws back its fangs in a long hiss. They look like sharp needles, needles about to rake into my flesh. And through my bones. I scurry backward until I hit the closet.

The snake props its tail against the bed, recoils like a spring, and then flies through the air toward me.

A real live snake is *flying* at my face.

I'm paralyzed with fear and my brain struggles to process that information. I only have enough time to do one thing before I die. Scream? Faint? Close my eyes?

Fight! That command slices through my terror like a sharp knife. I'm not sure if it comes from Ahkai or in my head, but I know I can't die like this.

At the last second, I use my only weapon: the toilet bowl cleaner. The squirt of liquid hits the snake right in the eye. It falls to the ground and slithers under the bed. My entire body trembles with relief, and I know my feet will give out if I try to stand up.

Ahkai is on the opposite side of the bed, pressed against the window. We both stare at each other, panting, trying to control our panic. His eyes bulge out of the sockets, and he opens his mouth, but I put a trembling finger to my lips to shush him. That snake could shoot out from under the bed at any moment, and we need to listen for any noises.

I get a moment of déjà vu, back to yesterday when I was in the same position with Mariss. I inch closer to the door, hoping I can escape again. With my neck, I motion to Ahkai to come toward the door as well.

Then, I notice a movement along the ceiling.

"Watch out!" I warn him in the nick of time. Ahkai ducks and the snake flies over his head, slamming into the windowpane, then dropping to the ground.

Ahkai tries to run to me, but as usual, he falls over his own legs and lands on the bed.

"Ahkai!" I scream, and rush to help him. But there is no way I can get to him before the snake does.

Ahkai lets out a battle cry and flings himself toward the snake on the ground. I cover my face with my hands. I can't watch.

Silence.

I peek through my fingers. I'm shaking, afraid to peer around the bed and see a snake wrapped around my best friend's neck.

Then, Ahkai gets to his feet. He seems fine, though he's trembling, and his glasses are hanging from his nose. He clutches his heaving chest with his hand.

I peep over the bed and see the whittling knife slammed into the snake's head. There is no blood, just yellow goo dripping from the fangs.

Ahkai grabs the bag with the cleaner and strides toward the door, not even bothering to fix his glasses.

"Now do you believe me?" I shriek. "Where're you going?"

"To alert the authorities!"

I glance at the brass comb on the floor. The spiral markings are gone, and it looks like it's been dropped in hot lava. I brush it with my finger; it's not hot at all. I push the comb into my pocket and follow Ahkai downstairs, still terrified, but relieved to have him as an ally.

"Good afternoon, Fairy Vale Police Station," drawls a tired male voice.

Ahkai opens his mouth, but no sound comes out.

"Good afternoon?" the voice repeats in an irritated tone.

I grab the phone. "Hello, my name is Josephine. My Daddy's girlfriend is a monster!"

"Sorry, sweetie, I can't help yuh. My girlfriend is a monster too." The policeman chuckles and hangs up the phone.

I stare at the receiver and back at Ahkai, whose face is to the ground. I'm not sure what to do, but then Ahkai lifts his head and looks me dead in the eyes.

"I am going to make snake repellent." With squared shoulders, he does his soldier march into the kitchen.

I'm still shaken, sitting at the kitchen table, trembling. I marvel at Ahkai, who stirs a mixture of olive oil, cinnamon, and cloves in a pot. He gets palpitations if he has to talk to a stranger but can hum over a stove after being attacked by a supernatural snake . . .

I glance outside, hoping to see Jalopy in the distance. After I show Daddy the dead snake with a knife jammed into its head and explain the significance of the comb, we have to return it during the full moon tonight. I hope Daddy remembers exactly where he fished it out of the sea. In the meantime, I pray that no more of Mariss's pets show up.

Ahkai's concoction smells delicious, and I'm not sure how it is a repellent, until he adds the mixture to the toilet bowl cleaner. He shakes the bottle and heads outside.

I follow him, and as an afterthought, I grab a big bag of rice from the kitchen cupboard. Ahkai sprays the fluid along all the doors and windows. As an extra safety measure, I pour rice along the entrances too. Ahkai points out the spots that I miss; the mythology doesn't seem so ridiculous to him now.

When we're done, we bow our heads and recite the Lord's Prayer.

It's after three p.m., and normally the air would be filled with the chatter of our classmates walking home from school, but everyone is secured in their homes, locked down, waiting for the storm to pass.

Everyone except our parents.

We're in the living room, eyes peeled on the road through the window. There's still no sign of Miss Mo or Daddy. I punch Daddy's number into the phone, over and over again, hoping to hear the sound of his voice.

"Maybe we should go to my house," says Ahkai.

"I have to be here when Daddy comes home," I point

out. "He needs to know the truth, and fast." Ahkai nods, but swallows.

"It's okay, Ahkai, you can go home if you want." I hope I sound brave. To my relief, Ahkai shakes his head and remains seated.

It's almost four now, but outside is so dreary from the thunderclouds it seems like six. We leave a message on Miss Mo's voicemail demanding that she comes over to Daddy's straightaway.

Five o'clock, and still no sign of Daddy. I start to get worried. He needs to get home so we can return the comb to Mariss's lair before she discovers our plan. Behind the thunderclouds, the sun sets. The sky looks like it's on fire, the deep red and gold a beautiful warning of the pending storm.

In the distance, there is a silhouette. The big afro looks like a miniature sun going below the horizon. The hips sway from side to side, like the dance of a cobra for a snake charmer.

Mariss.

CHAPTER 22

Ahkai is armed with another knife, so I grab a large chopping knife from the kitchen drawer.

Thumb over or under fingers? I shift my grip on the handle, trying to find the best hold to defend myself. The thought of using the blade makes me sick. I'm not sure if I'm capable of plunging it into someone's flesh, even if that someone isn't human. I say another silent prayer for the repellent to work so I don't have to find out.

Mariss glides up the path to the house. I look at her, covered in long-sleeved clothing, and remember Ahkai telling me that fish and snakes are cold-blooded.

No wonder she never sweats...

Mariss passes the hibiscus bush and comes up the stairs, her heels hitting the pavement. I stare at her feet, wondering how someone with an anaconda bottom learned to walk so confidently in heels.

She's almost at the door. She takes out her house keys from her bag.

It didn't work.

Then, she staggers back from the step. Her chin pops up in the air, so quick that if I had blinked, I would have missed the movement. She sniffs the air, like how she sniffed the fish food so many weeks ago, but this time she gags.

"Yes!" whispers Ahkai. Mariss's head snaps toward us, and her eyes turn yellow. Ahkai and I yelp in unison and jump back from the window.

"Josie Sweets," hisses Mariss. I am so scared that my hands start to shake. "Josie Sweets, what did you do? You naughty girl! And is that Ahkai in there? Ahkai, cutie, come outside to me."

Ahkai holds his knife in front of him, his hand shaking as well.

Mariss laughs and inhales. "Rice? You cooking pelau?" She lets out a loud cackle. It's a far cry from her regular, high-pitched giggle. It's cold and sharp, like jagged ice.

"Cloves? Sulfur? Cinnamon? I hate cinnamon!" Mariss says the word "cinnamon" as if it were the most disgusting thing in the world.

I turn to look at my mother's picture on the TV stand, forgetting it's no longer there. Mariss never brought it back from "the cleaners."

A jolt of anger surges through me.

"Josie Sweets, I'm not going to hurt you," says Mariss. "I could have killed both of you today when you were following me. It's Vincent I got a problem with. Asking me about moving out? He will get what coming to him." Daddy still spoke to her about leaving, even after I asked him not to! Why oh why didn't he listen?

I forget that Mariss could probably crush me with her pinkie. "Leave him alone!" I shout.

Mariss doesn't answer. Then, a piercing melody penetrates the air. I recognize the strange words from the song at Ramona's wedding. Ahkai's eyes glaze over, and he drops the knife. He takes shaky steps toward the side door.

"Ahkai! What are you doing?!" I yank on his arm, trying to pull him back. It's like restraining a tank with a rope.

I hold on to the dining table with my other hand. That manages to slow him, but my palms slide down his arm, to his hand, now his fingers.

The force of the release causes me to fall back onto the table. Ahkai stumbles a bit, but then continues toward the side door. Mariss does a climbing riff. It reawakens the memory of a building wave, about to splash on top of my head. I cover my ears. She's trying to mess with my mind.

I run in front of Ahkai and attempt to push him back from the door. He swats me away like a fly, and I tumble to the ground. When did he get this strong?

He's reaching for the doorknob now. I need to break him out of Mariss's trance! Otherwise he'll walk right into her eager, poisonous arms. There's one thing I can think of. I pray that it works.

I yell his name and clap at the same time, slamming my hands together so hard it stings. "Alpha Mike! Alpha Mike! Alpha Mike! Alpha Mike!" I stop before the fifth cry.

"Alpha Mike!" Ahkai is brought out of the trance with his own clap. He jerks like he's been slapped around the head, lets out a choking sound, and scrambles away from the door. He fumbles with the knife on the floor, shaking so hard he can barely keep the weapon in his hand.

Mariss cuts off her long note, and then it's silent.

Ahkai and I look at each other, unsure of what to do next. I want my daddy! But suppose he comes home right at this moment? What will Mariss do to him?

CRASH!

Ahkai and I scream and dive to the floor.

"Josie, stop playing cricket in the house!"

Mariss has thrown a rock through the newly repaired kitchen window. We peep outside and see Mariss, her arms folded and a frozen smile on her face. She stares at the side door, not moving.

Where is Daddy?

Ahkai runs to the phone to call for help. He presses the buttons, and then looks at me, shaking his head.

There is no dial tone.

Outside seems to get dark within minutes. Mariss is just standing there, eyes still fixed on the door. The thunder booms again, and the rain starts to fall.

"You can't keep me out for much longer," she says in a singsong voice. "If you beg, I'll let you say goodbye to your daddy."

She has to be bluffing . . . she has to be. *Daddy is okay. Daddy is okay. Daddy is okay.* But deep inside, I know he's not okay. He should be home by now. He *always* comes home. Something is very very wrong.

Ahkai gasps. "The rain will wash away the repellent!"

We look at each other in horror and rush up the stairs. We slam my bedroom door, but when I go to lock it, I remember it's broken.

"The drawers!"

Ahkai and I put down the knives and struggle to push the chest of drawers in front of the door. Facing the door, we pick up the knives, our hands quavering, and move backward until we reach the bed in the middle of the room.

I sit down on the tube of Benjie's Balm.

Suddenly, I remember how Mariss retreated from a little bit of the vapor rub on my daddy's knees.

"Put out your hands," I say to Ahkai. I squeeze the tube and rub the ointment all over his body, careful not to let any of the balm get into his eyes. I have to twist the tube to get enough to cover my hands and neck, and as an afterthought, I rub some of the ointment on the white ribbon in my hair.

The rain slams against the roof. It pummels down so hard it rattles the window.

Mariss could get inside the house any minute. My hand starts to get tired from holding the heavy knife in the air.

She could already be in here.

A high-pitched wail of anguish comes from Daddy's bedroom.

She's inside . . . and she's found her pet.

I remember Mrs. Edgecombe's warning. *Don't piss*

them off, hear? Make amends! I wish I could burst into dust and disappear.

Then, something hits into my bedroom door. Ahkai and I flinch and press ourselves against the bed. The heavy drawers move forward an inch. Mariss screeches with anger and slams against the door again. A crack appears in the wood. It won't hold for much longer. Ahkai and I brace ourselves for battle.

We wait, but there's nothing. We look at each other, confused. Maybe Mariss has given up?

CRASH!

The noise comes from behind us!

We turn to see Mariss's upper body protruding through the window. Her face hasn't transformed like it did at the reserve, but she still looks monstrous, with her features twisted with pure rage and pieces of glass jutting out from her cheeks. Her hands clench on to the windowsill.

Ahkai lets out his battle cry and throws his knife at Mariss. It hurtles through the air, heading right toward the spiral pendant on her chest.

Mariss catches the knife with one hand before it touches her, its pointy end just about to graze the pendant. Then, she lifts the other hand from the windowsill and pops the glass from her face like they're pimples. Ahkai and I gasp in shock and fear.

Time stops.

How is she balancing from two stories high?

Her snake body.

Her midsection twists from side to side under the dress. The spiral pendant hanging from her neck quivers.

Mariss hurls the knife back at us, and we dive to the floor. The knife hits the chest of drawers and goes right in to the hilt.

Ahkai and I press our backs to the bed and wait for our imminent death. We hear a loud thud as the creature hits the bedroom floor. Snake-Mariss sounds as heavy as a boulder. Ahkai reaches for my hand, and we hold on to each other tightly.

"Mariss, I'm so sorry! I didn't mean for any of this to happen. We can work this out," I plead, mucus building in my nose. Begging is my last resort. I don't want to die.

"Liar! You never accepted me before. Why would you now? But I told you I'd take care of your father, remember. I always keep my promises, Josie Sweets."

The final "s" sound in "sweets" doesn't seem to end. I

tighten my grip on the chopping knife. I intend to go down fighting.

The bed sinks in from her weight. The sheets rustle as she comes closer and closer. Ahkai's breathing becomes short and choppy.

She's almost above us, and I take a deep breath, squeezing the handle and getting ready to swing. A line of Benjie's-scented sweat rolls down my forehead. I expect to feel sharp claws tearing at my head any second.

Mariss hisses, and then gags. The weight moves from off the bed, and we hear another loud thud.

Then nothing.

Ahkai and I look at each other, and together we cautiously peep over the bed.

The curtain by the broken window flaps in the windy rain.

Mariss is gone.

CHAPTER 23

I jump up with a throbbing pain in my neck and gasp, thinking Mariss has sunk her fangs into my flesh, but it's just Ahkai's elbow jammed into my neck.

We must have passed out in the bathtub. We were both too scared to leave the house, so we locked ourselves in the bathroom and sprayed the floor with the cleaner, flea powder, repellent—anything we had. The only thing left is the margarine; we ate the leftover chicken before I took first watch.

From the window, the moon shimmers bright and full in the sky.

Daddy!

I scramble out of the tub, causing Ahkai to fall and bang his head. I unlock the door and rush into his room.

"Daddy?"

He's not here. I inch to the other side of the bed . . . and the snake is gone.

I push past Ahkai at the door and rush downstairs, yelling for Daddy over and over again. I step over some broken glass on the floor and grab the phone. *Dial tone.* I punch in Daddy's cell number and it goes straight to voicemail.

He's gone.

Mariss wouldn't have drowned him. My heart refuses to accept that. She must have chosen Daddy as her once-in-a-lifetime mate and taken him to her underwater lair. I struggle with the many emotions erupting inside me: shock, anger, and fear. I sway on the spot, and if it weren't for Ahkai, I would fall to the ground.

He gently guides me down on the bottom stairs.

Then, there is a loud bang. We leap to our feet and scramble up the stairs to the bathroom.

But it's only Miss Mo at the door.

"What gine on in here?" she says, looking up at us. "I get catch in the storm so had to wait a few hours by Valerie."

"Mummy!" Ahkai runs toward her. She is startled but still puts her arm around him. It's rare to see Ahkai show such emotion. As much as he bickers and is embarrassed

254

by Miss Mo's quirks, when he's upset, he always finds comfort in her arms.

Watching Ahkai and Miss Mo embrace is too much for me to handle, and I lose all composure. My heart aches so much for someone to hold me like that, the pain forms a hard bubble in my chest. I start to hyperventilate. I don't want to take charge anymore; I just want to hide my face in someone's skirt and pretend my worries are gone, even if it's only for a few minutes.

"Jo? What happen?" Miss Mo reaches out to me. I hurry to seek solace in the folds in her skirt. She smells of dishwashing liquid and fish cakes. She brings me closer to her and gently rubs my back. I close my eyes and a little bit of tension unravels inside.

"Where Vince?"

Ahkai and I start talking at the same time. Miss Mo looks down at us with a cynical expression that mirrors Ahkai's—at least the Ahkai before we were attacked by a mystical snake creature.

"Hol' on! Hol' on! Mumma what? Look, one person talk at a time." I spill my guts to Miss Mo, telling her about what happened at the Wildlife Reserve, the conversation with Mrs. Edgecombe, and the deadly events this evening.

Miss Mo is pensive. She rests a crooked finger under

her nose. Ahkai and I wait for her to tell us the next line of attack. I think we should call the Barbados Defence Force or maybe the Task Force. Surely Mariss would be no match against the men dressed in black with the huge high-powered guns.

"Now listen, don't think I didn't know what was gine on," says Miss Mo. I lean forward in anticipation. *She has a plan!*

"I know it was only you and your father before, but you got to give Mariss a chance. She is a good woman."

It's like DJ Hypa Tension did one of his "pull up" sound effects in the kitchen.

What!

Miss Mo doesn't believe me. She's the one adult who I hoped would convince others to help find the lair, but Miss Mo, who believes in duppies, small men who live in bottles, and the power of black-eyed peas, doesn't believe me. The irony is so great that I erupt into hysterical laughter.

"But, Mum, Jo is telling the truth." Ahkai looks like he's about to cry.

"Hush now, the Lord ain' gine let nothing happen to Vince, but I gine call the coast guard in case he get catch in the storm too."

She grips our hands and leads us back to her house

while complaining about the damage the storm did to her stalls and how much money it will cost to fix them.

I stare at her with amazement while she's on the phone with the coast guard. It's like a dog chasing the wheel of a car. The dog doesn't really expect to catch it; if the car stops moving, the dog retreats and runs back home. People like to believe in things until they have to face them.

I want to scream the truth over Miss Mo's shoulder, but it wouldn't make a difference. No one believes me . . . except Ahkai. He's seated at the kitchen table, rocking back and forth in the chair.

While still on the phone, Miss Mo puts a box of Frosted Flakes, milk, and three bowls on the table, but the thought of food turns my stomach. I watch as Ahkai eats the Frosted Flakes one by one, dipping each flake into a bowl of milk for two seconds before chewing it.

How can I eat knowing my daddy is missing? I know that Mariss has captured him; I hope she hasn't—I can't finish the thought.

The brass comb in my back pocket presses into my skin. I shift to the side and pull it out, rubbing its burnt surface with my thumb.

Miss Mo hangs up. "All right, them gine look into it, but this storm was a killer." She grabs canned goods from her cupboard and throws them into a box. "A lotta people need help, so I going down to the shelter."

She moves across the kitchen curtain, looking outside as if she expects Daddy to pull up outside in Jalopy. "Wunna stay here in case the coast guard call back."

Miss Mo lifts the box and rubs Ahkai on the head. "Ahkai, take care of Jo." He sits up in his chair and nods.

Then she pats my cheek. "Don't worry, Jo. Vince always comes home. He know he got a lil girl to take care of."

I push my bowl away and look at my house through the window. With the broken kitchen and bedroom windows, it resembles a neglected, abandoned building.

Miss Mo sighs behind me, and then the door closes. It is quiet.

The full moon emerges from behind the clouds.

I know what I have to do. I'm going to return the comb and save my daddy.

"There is nothing I can do to stop you, is there?" Ahkai says, reading my mind again. He doesn't wait for an answer and gets up as if he's always been ready for battle.

We fill a backpack with the few potential weapons we can find in the bathroom—a waterproof flashlight, a container of Vicks VapoRub, and a bag of Epsom salts. Then, we head to the beach.

The night is deadly quiet; there is no wind, no crickets, not even the echo of a barking dog. It's like every creature in Fairy Vale is tense and holding their breath, waiting to see if we will survive this encounter. I wish I could turn back to the safety of Ahkai's house, but I have a gut feeling that my daddy is alive and praying for help.

We get to the top of Coconut Hill and I pause, looking out at the darkness of the sea. The shadow of the silk cotton tree is haunting in the moonlight. It wasn't long ago I was here at this spot, upset about not getting on the cricket team and certain that I had been cursed with the worst life in the world. I would give anything to go back to that time.

We come to the junction at the bottom of Coconut Hill—the place where Mariss disappeared when we tried to follow her. There are two main access points to the beach. We always go left, through the fish market, which is the calmer side of the beach. But it's possible that Mariss went the other direction, where there is a larger beach but much rougher waters.

"Which path should we take?" Ahkai whispers.

"Alas!"

Ahkai and I scream out and hold on to each other. We turn to see Casper, squatting behind a huge rock in front of a streetlight.

"Everything seems calm, but these humanlings can sense the danger that awaits them. Now they're at a crossroads. Will they make the right choice? Little do they know that what they seek lies where the Caribbean Sea meets the Atlantic Ocean."

"Casper! Do you know where Mariss's lair is?" I ask, both annoyed and excited to see him. "The vile vixen!"

"I've been spotted!" Casper ducks behind the rock. I move toward it, determined to wrangle understandable English from him, but it's too late. He's jumped over a crumbling wall and is dashing toward the fish market.

"Let's go after him!" I cry, but Ahkai shakes his head.

"He told us all we need to know." He beckons for me to follow and turns right.

We crawl through a small space between sea grape trees, shining the flashlight ahead of us. It opens out onto a clear area on a cliff. After I refused to get back into a boat, Daddy would bring me here to lie on the grass and watch him throw the net out from *Joanne*.

The sea is violent, with the tide extra high from the

storm. I can barely hear the sound of my thoughts over the waves crashing against the shore. My heart thumps against my chest at the idea of venturing into the murderous waters.

Ahkai points to a rock in the sea—a rock shaped like a fist—a rock that is haunted. The place where the Caribbean Sea meets the Atlantic Ocean . . .

Thank you, Casper.

A flock of birds flutters up from the fist-shaped rock into the sky. We strain our eyes, staring into the dark water, looking for any sign of Mariss.

"Let's get a closer look," I say, and we go back through the bush to head onto the beach. My mind is racing, trying to decide on our next move.

Should we wait for Mariss to appear? Should we try to get help?

I notice a glimmer from the tall shrubs that grow along the shore. I shine the flashlight at the spot, and half-covered in the vines is Jalopy.

My heart skips a beat, and time slows down.

"Please, please, please." I run toward the car and shine the light inside. There's no one there, and to my relief, no sign of blood.

My heart starts beating again. I try to calm down, but now I know my daddy is here, and he is in trouble.

I shine the light around the area until I see her—parked along the shore with the other boats. *Joanne.*

I remove my sneakers. Ahkai is already shaking his head. "No no no no NO!"

"I have to help Daddy." I grab the bag from him, take out the Vicks VapoRub, and rub it all over my body.

Ahkai launches into a long monologue while I'm applying the ointment. "We cannot do this! We are not prepared. The menthol is not as active in this product. There is no guarantee it will repel the creature! It is better for us to seek help, or wait until a pharmacy is—"

He's right. The smell isn't as strong as the Benjie's, so I apply a second layer, using the rest of the ointment in the container.

"And what can we do with Epsom Epsom Epsom Epsom Epsom salts?! Magnesium sulfate has many uses, including anti-inflammatory properties, muscle relaxant, laxative yes, but only if ingested. How will you get Mariss to swallow it? We need a plan!"

I ignore him and start pushing *Joanne* toward the water. She is small, but still very heavy. She's moving forward only a foot at a time, but I will stay out here all night if I have to. I clench my jaw in determination.

After a few seconds, Ahkai helps me push. The sand gets colder and damper under our feet, and soon we are close to the edge of the sea. I gasp when the water first rolls over my foot. It's strange but I feel comforted. The waves hit hard five times, as if applauding my return to the sea.

I turn to Ahkai. "You have to go get help, okay?"

He closes his eyes and starts to rock. "I can't! I can't! I can't—"

"No, Ahkai! Listen to me," I say, shaking him. "I need you to go get help. The police station isn't far away. You can do this! This is Operation SOS. Come in, Alpha Mike!"

Ahkai steels his shoulders, opens his eyes, and nods. "Over."

I give Ahkai a big hug, and he doesn't push me away. We cling to each other, knowing it could be our last.

Then I pull away and hop into *Joanne*. Though it's been years since I've been in her, it feels familiar, like I've returned home. I yank on the starter rope, just as Daddy taught me so long ago, and the engine splutters to life. Reciting all of Daddy's instructions in my head, I pull the tiller in the direction of the rock.

I'm coming, Daddy.

I can hear Ahkai shouting, "Be safe, Juliette Charlie!" over and over again.

CHAPTER 24

The water is choppy so it is difficult to keep *Joanne* on course for the rock. I am terrified the boat will capsize; it comes dangerously close to toppling over several times. I'm already drenched and shivering but I stay on course. I have to return the comb to Mariss's lair and free Daddy.

"All right, girl, keep steady," I say. Daddy says *Joanne* is the true spirit of Mum because she always pushes forward when you need her to. He says he's had several long conversations with her while out at sea.

The wind blasts through my wet cornrows, and my teeth chatter. Daddy's not here now. There's no light up ahead. I'm alone in the dark ocean.

Joanne is the closest thing I have to someone's skirt . . .

My chest starts to burn again, and I push my fist against it, rubbing to ease the pressure. I close my eyes, listening to the breathing of the ocean, and inhale. The salty sea spray flushes away the tension inside. And then, just like that, words fall from my mouth.

I'm talking to my mummy.

"One time I call Daddy's phone, and he ain' answer. I call over and over again, and the longer he took to answer the phone, the more anxious I got. Turns out it was on silent, and he was all right, but I had nightmares for days after. You went to bed and never woke up. Just like that. No goodbye or nothing. You left me and almost took Daddy with you."

The sea seems to be eavesdropping on our conversation. The water is calmer, and the waves rock the boat like a mother's arms. *Joanne* moves forward with ease.

"When Daddy's with a woman, I worry she'll leave and make him sad, or worse. I just don't want anyone to come and hurt us all over again. I'm scared all the time . . . except when I'm bowling."

I make the bowling action with my arm, out toward the rock in the ocean. "Bet you'd want me on the cricket team, wouldn't you, Mummy? You'd cheer for me.

You won't stop me from playing just because I could get hurt."

It's like Mummy's voice breaks through the clouds and whispers the revelation in my head from heaven.

I'm doing the same thing to Daddy . . .

I stroke the peeling red paint on the bow, then release a heavy sigh.

"I get it."

It is like deadweight has been lifted from my shoulders. I wonder if this is how the churchgoers feel after Pastor Williams dunks them in the water at baptism.

A vicious wave brings me back to reality. The tide has returned in a wild rage. I have to pull the tiller all the way to the right to get *Joanne* back in the direction of the rock.

I ignore the urge to return to shore and shine the flashlight out toward the rock.

I'm almost there. The bad news is that it's just a large rock—there's nowhere to walk or dock the boat. I was hoping it would be like a small island, but that isn't the case.

Turn back! my brain screams at me. *This doesn't make any sense!* But my gut urges me to go forward. *Joanne* splutters, and then with a groan, the engine dies.

"Please, God, no." I yank the rope again and again,

but it does not start. She must be out of fuel. I shine my light around the boat, hoping to see the red bottle with fuel on board.

Nothing.

The waves pull me out farther into the ocean, away from the rock.

It's so close . . . a few meters more.

I weigh my options: Swim and stay on the rock until help comes, or drift away in the ocean with only Epsom salts to survive on.

I secure the flashlight on my wrist and look down at the water, dark and menacing, and I feel anxiety building inside. I have flashbacks of the sea pulling me away from shore and my body fighting to reach the surface. My feet are paralyzed, refusing to move, but the longer I take, the farther away the boat drifts from the rock. I close my eyes and think about Daddy singing reggae and doing his corny dance.

Goodbye, Joanne.

I take the leap.

My mind panics as soon as the cold water closes over me, and it is a struggle to stay calm. I push through the water, trying to get as much distance as possible before I come up for breath, but I don't last long. Something latches itself around my toe, and I scream out, taking in a mouthful of salt water. I break the surface and suck in the air, making gasping, sobbing sounds, then yank the thing from my toe—it's only seaweed.

While I inhale and exhale, trying to get hold of myself, the tide pulls me farther from the rock. I breathe in as much air as I can and dive again.

This time, I am much calmer, and I shine the flashlight forward. I can see the rock ahead. It is so large I can't see the bottom of it.

My lungs start to burn, and I am about to surface when I hear a foreign tune.

Mariss.

My fear seems to burn the little oxygen I have left, and I scramble up for air. As soon as my head breaks the surface, the sound disappears. I take in another deep breath, but before I can dive again, a wave covers my head.

I flail underwater for a bit before regaining my form, and swim toward the sound. There is a large opening in the rock, and I head toward it, the sound getting louder and louder.

The edges of the rocks are sharp, and I struggle to swim through the opening without brushing its sides. My foot hits against a pointy rock, and I can't help but gulp in pain. Salt water rushes down my throat.

I need air!

I don't know how long the tunnel is, but I swim harder, the pressure from my lungs overshadowing the pain from hitting the jagged rock. I am about to burst when the space widens, and I'm able to swim upward.

My lungs are on fire! I kick my legs hard and push my arms through the water.

Just when I think I can go no farther, my nose breaks the surface. I can breathe! I spend a few seconds coughing and taking in precious air.

When I regain my senses, I realize I'm in a large cave. Unlike the tunnel, the cave walls are smooth and crystal blue, similar to glass that has been sanded down and varnished. The stalactites are pure white, like oblong, jagged teeth, and a warm glow radiates from the beehive-shaped stalagmites on the cave floor.

It makes no sense! A cave in the middle of a rock? Mariss's echo is gentle here, much softer than outside the rock. It's like the walls are absorbing most of the sound.

I pull myself out of the water, and the heat of the cave encircles me, like I'm sitting in front of a warm bonfire. The salt water has already washed the vapor rub from my skin. Ahkai was right; my first line of defense is gone and I haven't even faced Mariss yet.

The stalagmites form a path around the corner, like fairy lights in a garden. I follow the way, careful not to touch any of the structures in case they set off some kind of magical alarm.

I turn the corner and almost walk off the short ledge. Down below, sitting on a giant rock shaped like an ice cream cone in the middle of a crystal-blue-green pool, is Mariss.

Her afro is as big as a sea fan. A white mesh cloth floats around her body, even though there is no wind in the cave. The brass spiral pendant is larger than ever, almost covering her entire upper torso.

I jump back around the corner, bend low to the ground, and take another peek.

"Come," hisses Mariss. My heart leaps.

She's seen me!

But Daddy steps out of the shadows. I have to stop myself from screaming out his name. *He's alive!* His eyes are focused on Mariss, and his face is still, like it's carved from rock. He is shirtless, and the spiral mark on his chest glows. Mariss starts to sing again, low at first, but the higher her voice gets, the brighter the mark shines.

Mariss throws her head back and spreads her arms wide. The water starts to ripple, and then dozens of lionfish leap out of the water, their venomous brown-and-yellow needle spines making large splashes.

She reaches the climax of the song, and the spiral pendant starts to wiggle. I know what is coming next, but I'm still not prepared when the black-and-gold snake bursts from the pendant and slithers around her shoulders. It's at least four times bigger than the one that attacked me and Ahkai in the bedroom. The snake still doesn't detach itself from Mariss, and I realize the end of the snake's tail is buried inside her chest.

It's a part of her...

I remember the spiral pendant I wore around my neck. *What if a snake is inside me?* I suppress the urge to vomit.

The snake wraps itself around Mariss's neck, and its forked tongue darts out against her face. She caresses its head like it's a newborn baby.

Then, Mariss's eyes turn bright yellow. The skin along the side of her face starts to shrivel, like the bottom of a lit cigarette, until the skin turns into glittering green-and-blue scales along her cheeks. The transformation continues along her body, covering her breasts and down the sides of her upper torso.

It's mesmerizing and terrifying all at once.

Her legs seem to melt into each other like hot

wax, and then they twist into a thick snake form with black-and-gold diagonal stripes, with the tail hanging off the rock and swinging from side to side. She shines like she's been doused in olive oil.

I stare in horror at the sight in front of me, a scream building in my throat. Mariss sings a different tune—like the one she sang to Ahkai—and Daddy starts to walk toward her. As he gets near the pool, the fish grow still and seem to form a row for him to walk through.

"Daddy!" I cry out. He stops walking. Although his face doesn't change expression, his hanging arms twitch, so I believe he's heard me.

Mariss snaps her head around. "Josie Sweets!"

The snake around her neck uncurls itself and turns to me, its tongue flicking in my direction.

"If I had known you were coming, I would have made myself more presentable." She stresses the "s" in "presentable" and pats her afro.

"Please," I beg, my voice cracking. I swallow and try again. "Please, Mariss, please don't hurt him."

"What more you want from me, Josephine?" Mariss's yellow eyes flash brighter. "He accepted my gift. That was his choice, but you see ..." she says, wagging her finger. The snake mimics her motion with its head.

"This is what I get for being too generous. I was patient and let him put you first—I get it, you're as damaged as he was. But then he had the nerve to brush me aside for another woman!"

"But he didn't!" I cry, but she ignores me, looking at Daddy like he's a piece of gray slime at the bottom of a dirty bucket.

"Come!" she demands, and Daddy moves closer to the edge of the pool.

"No!" I try to climb down but my foot slips on the rocks. I roll to the bottom, hitting my head on the gravelly floor.

My vision is blurred for a few seconds. I touch my forehead and wince. A trickle of blood runs down from the gash.

"Please, Daddy's done nothing wrong," I beg in a weak voice.

"Nothing? Nothing!" Mariss rants. "I gave him everything—wealth, health, spoiled him with love! I saved his life! And as soon as he's satisfied he tells me he's sorry I have to leave? Men are so ungrateful, and this one almost had me fooled."

"Wait—no," I protest, but Mariss is lost in anger. One eager lionfish breaks from the row and flips into the air.

"When he called out to me he had nothing. His pain consumed him! I could taste it in his blood. He hated his life."

I hate my life.

I'm bowled over by memories of me scratching the "J" into the silk cotton tree on Coconut Hill with the rock, the drop of blood seeping into the silk cotton tree's bark, and my scream of pain and frustration. If Miss Mo is right, and spirits live in that silk cotton tree, then I may have released Mariss when I cut into it.

"Oh no," I whisper.

I shake my head, hoping it's not true, but all the evidence is right there in front of me. Daddy had his fang nightmare the same day I cut into the tree, and Mariss appeared the next day. How jittery Mariss acted when she was near the silk cotton tree. Her outrage for animals trapped in cages—like she knew what it felt like to be trapped. It all leads back to the tree, and I was too selfish and distracted to notice.

"Please, wait!" I push myself up, then a sharp pain in my knee brings me back to the ground.

Daddy steps inside the pool. It's about a foot deep. The excited lionfish break the surface again, this time opening their mouths in silent screams. Their toxic spines glisten with poison, ready to paralyze Daddy so that even as the water floods his lungs, he won't be able to move a muscle.

Mariss starts singing again, and the snake moves down to her chest and curls up between her breasts.

It's all my fault.

I did this. I'm responsible for bringing Mariss into my home, and I have to be the one to make things right.

I force myself up on one knee and then drag my body to its feet. "No, you could taste it in *my* blood! It was me! I released you from the tree!"

There is a chilling silence.

Mariss's eyes widen and fade to a milky yellow. The lionfish grow still in the water and Daddy stops wading through the pool.

I pull the white ribbon from my hair and press it against the cut on my forehead, then stumble close to the edge of the water, keeping the weight off the bad knee, and throw the ribbon in her direction. Of course, the ribbon falls into the pool. Mariss makes a gesture with her finger, and a bubble forms around the blood-stained cloth. I watch, openmouthed, as the bubble with the ribbon rises into the air and floats toward her.

She plucks the ribbon from the bubble and inhales.

Mariss shrieks and her eyes flash again—this time they're bright red.

I wince as I drop to my knees, and words tumble out like I'm at confession, spilling out all my sins faster than fish guts can fall from a bucket.

"And I was the one who forced him to dance with Miss Alleyne at the wedding. He didn't want to! And he told me he really wanted things to work out between the two of you, and I didn't let him. And he didn't even go to the hospital to visit Miss Alleyne 'cause he knew you'd be upset. And I'm the one who lied and said you were leaving. He didn't want you to go! It was all me! I'm so sorry!"

I take a breath. So, I stretched the truth at the end, but who cares. *I need to save my daddy.*

"I should kill you," Mariss says, crushing the ribbon in her hand. The snake lifts its head higher in the air and sways to a silent rhythm.

I remember Mrs. Edgecombe saying a Sea Mumma takes cares of those who worship her. *Maybe I can appeal to Mariss's better nature.*

"Just please, let my daddy go," I beg again. "He loved you! He told me so all the time. He said you were—you were—you were the best thing that ever happened to him. You were like—like—dumplings in his soup!"

I wish I had more experience sucking up.

Mariss stares at me for a few seconds, then her eyes fade from red to white. The snake settles itself around her shoulders.

"Very well."

I let out a strangled sob and rush into the pool before she changes her mind. The water almost melts my skin. I pull on Daddy's hand but he's like a wall.

"Leave!" Mariss commands, and her eyes flash. The mark burns like fire on Daddy's chest. His body relaxes, and I'm finally able to move him. I put his arm around my shoulder and guide him out of the pool.

"Where are you going?" Mariss's menacing tone makes the hair on my arms stand up. "We agreed your daddy could leave . . . not you. A sacrifice must be made."

My heart drops to my feet, and my throat goes dry. I don't want to risk arguing and anger her even more. My mind races, trying to think of a plan to get me out of this, but I come up with nothing. I won't ever see my home again, Ahkai, Miss Mo, never bowl another cricket ball or taste another nutmeg pancake . . . it's too horrible to accept, but I don't have a choice. I need to take responsibility.

I kiss Daddy's arm before removing it from my shoulder.

"I love you, Daddy. I'm so sorry. Please forgive me."

I turn to Mariss, accepting my fate. Mariss looks down at me with her smug expression and strokes the snake. She starts to hum, and its forked tongue darts out, licking her finger.

Daddy takes three steps forward, wobbles on the fourth, and then stops walking.

I'm worried that he's trapped in his silent space till I see his fingers fold into a fist.

He's fighting it!

"Leave, Daddy!" I yell in frustration. I try to push him from the water.

Mariss's pitch gets higher and higher, and the snake around her twists like a rubber band, but Daddy only twitches, never moving from the spot.

Mariss drops off in mid-note with a snarl. "Clearly he does not want to go."

"No, wait!" I cry. "H-He doesn't want to leave *you*, not me." But she doesn't buy it.

"Enough lies!" Her face is bent in fury. "I ain' got time for this!"

Through the clear water, the lionfish work like a pack of wolves, surrounding Daddy. Their mouths open and close, as if asking Mariss for permission to strike.

In a desperate move, I pull the Epsom salts from my bag.

"You and this salt thing again?" Mariss laughs.

Ignoring her, I rip the bag open and fling the salts as far as I can. The crystals scatter in the pool like hard droplets of rain, and the lionfish suck some of the particles into their mouths.

Mariss slowly slithers her snake body down the rock, her torso still upright. "Sorry, Josie Sweets, but I gave you too many chances to—"

Mariss pauses and looks down into the water.

The lionfish are twisting and swimming about in a circle. White worms slide out from under their back fins. As they wriggle, the worms get longer and longer, and then I realize they aren't worms. If those fish could talk, they would scream the same terrible noises that Ahkai's cousin made in the bathroom.

Mariss hisses and slithers up the rock before the water can touch the fish scales on her upper body. Just like at the zoo, her nose and mouth extend, and she bares her fangs at me.

I rush out of the water and try to yank Daddy from the pool, but he's too heavy.

"Impetus!" Mariss hisses, and the snake rises into an "S" shape. It catapults forward, detaching itself from her shiny

scales and leaving a small, dark hole between her breasts. The snake lands in the pool, and its wriggling body cuts through the water toward us.

"Daddy, please," I plead. I have no weapon to defend myself, and the snake is almost on us.

As Mariss cackles, pink, raw flesh moves up and down across the hole, like a blinking eye in the middle of her chest.

I close my eyes and clasp my hands to pray for a miracle. Something sharp pokes my hand.

Ahkai's lucky charm.

The snake shoots out of the water like a missile. Its fangs are long and pointy enough to shred my entire face. There's no doubt about it; it's going for the kill.

Time slows as I look at the pronged end of the hummingbird's tail, and then at the small hole in Mariss's chest. I get a flash of inspiration born out of pure terror.

I pop the wooden pendant from the chain and grip it between two fingers. I have one shot.

Focus. Precision. Speed.

Mariss is still consumed with laughter when I release the hummingbird from my grip. I watch as it hurtles through the air, and then I shield my face from the snake with my arm.

I have the pleasure of seeing the hummingbird meet

its target, its tail sinking right into the hole in Mariss's chest, just as the snake plunges its fangs into my hand.

We both cry out at the same time. She yanks the hummingbird from the hole, and a string of yellow goo shoots out from her chest. I watch as Mariss falls back behind the rock, before I drop to the ground.

The snake forces its fangs farther into my hand. My fear is greater than the actual pain of the bite; it feels like two needles are being slammed into my flesh.

Something jerks the snake away from me. I look up to see Daddy, crushing the snake with a large rock. He hits it over and over again like a man possessed.

There is no sign of Mariss. *We need to escape before she recovers.*

"Daddy!" I shout, and he looks at me with wild eyes. I try to stand, but my body doesn't respond. Daddy rushes over to me. I don't know if it's the venom, but a feeling of satisfaction sweeps over me, and I get the urge to sleep.

"We gotta stop the bleeding!" Daddy cries out in alarm and tries to rip a piece of his jeans off with his bare hands.

I remember Mum's handkerchief in my back pocket. I never took it out.

She's been with me the whole time . . .

"Pocket," I mumble. It comes out sounding like

"ploplack," but Daddy still understands. He searches my back pocket and pulls out Mariss's blackened comb. *I forgot all about it!* I open my mouth to tell him to return it, but my tongue feels as if it weighs ten pounds. I shift my eyes from the comb to the pool.

Daddy nods, and with a bowling action worth a place on any cricket team, he hurls the comb back into the blue-green water.

It's over . . .

I close my eyes, eager to finally get a good night's sleep.

"Bean, stay awake," Daddy urges. "Stay with me." He finds the handkerchief and ties it around my hand. Then he lifts me in his arms, climbing back up the rocks like he's some sort of gymnast.

Soon, I feel the coolness of water around me.

"'Old your breath, okay, Bean? Just like I taught you," Daddy says before diving into the water.

Somehow, he manages to get me through that narrow tunnel without even one bruise from the jagged rocks, but pain cuts through my body as soon as we break the surface. I gasp in agony and take in a breath at the same time, just before a gigantic wave crashes down on top of us.

The water whips us around like we're caught in a

tornado, ripping me from Daddy's arms. It's like the sea is going down a large drain, and Daddy and I are trapped in its intense currents, being sucked beneath the ocean's floor.

My mind screams for me to reach out for Daddy, but I have no control over my body. It's just me against the sea. Even if I did have strength, I am no match for a sea that's fighting back.

I think of Mum and wonder if this is how she felt the moment before she died, knowing she would be leaving all those she loved behind.

But at least we will all be in heaven, finally together as a family.

A wave of emotion builds inside me, and my head starts to hurt. Something is trapped inside my chest and trying to pound its way out. The more I resist, the more painful it becomes. I can't keep fighting it for much longer.

I am going to die.

Then, I let go. I exhale, and the pounding wave escapes from my heart. It moves up through my throat, passes my nose, swells in my brain, and then, salty tears flow from my eyes, becoming one with the sea.

I am crying.

As I'm pulled to the bottom of the ocean, I feel like

I'm being reborn. There's no stress—no burning in my lungs, ache in my head, or pain in my chest. It's like I'm drifting through the water like smoke dancing in the air.

I never want to leave the sea again.

I must be hallucinating, because silver-blue teardrops sparkle in the water above me. Bubbles form around them and they look like tiny stars in glass balls. The glowing bubbles form a line, attaching themselves to one another, and shoot to the bottom of the ocean.

Then, my body spasms, convulsing in the water. *Is this death?* More bubbles form around me and push me to the surface, like I'm wearing a foamy jetpack. I'm shocked by the unexpected presence of air, and I inhale while coughing up water.

"Bean!" Daddy appears, pulling me against his chest. "Daddy's 'ere."

I can't respond—now overwhelmed by pain. It feels like my blood is being replaced with fire. I want to plunge my body back under the sea.

"Don't cry, Bean," Daddy says, stroking my hair. "I gine never leave you again."

I hear loud sirens just before I pass out. *Thank you, Ahkai . . .*

Operation SOS was a success.

Over and out.

CHAPTER 25

I can't pretend I'm not jealous when the Fairy Vale cricket team walks out with the West Indies players. While David Rudder's "Rally 'round the West Indies" blares from the speakers, my schoolmates gawk up at the celebrity athletes; even Jared is starstruck.

Still, I'm lucky to be alive to see the match. Two months ago, the doctors at the hospital weren't sure the antivenom from Guyana would arrive in time.

The anthem ends with its high crescendo, and everyone in Kensington Oval cheers. I get teary-eyed when I look around at Daddy and Ahkai, hooting in their West Indies cricket shirts.

I take Mummy's handkerchief out of my pocket and dab the corners of my eyes. I cry at everything now, not just sad moments but happy moments too. Like if a couple is laughing over dinner, or when siblings hug and make up after a huge fight. Daddy almost banned me from watching Christmas movies—families singing carols around a tree is a guaranteed one-hour bawling session.

Now that my pipes are unclogged, it's difficult to control the flow of tears, but I don't mind. It feels good to let everything out.

"Did you know that Sir Garfield Sobers was only sixteen when he first played cricket for the West Indies in 1953?" Ahkai asks me. I didn't, and now it's one of my new goals. I have five years to train.

Ahkai is already nose deep in a book about the legendary batsman. I'm not sure the live match can pull his attention away from the pages, but I'm still glad he's somehow involved in the game. His forehead is shiny from layers of coconut oil Miss Mo applied to prevent more sunburn. Now that he's taking swimming classes twice a week, he's a shade darker.

Daddy reaches into our cooler for a cold soda. You can still see a faint outline of the spiral mark on his chest. At first, I was terrified he'd go searching for Mariss. I wondered if she allowed me to survive only to watch her take him away from me again, but he stayed by my side for the entire time at the hospital.

I remember how Daddy refused to leave the cave without me, and, of course, a tear runs down my cheek. I'm so thankful to be alive, and I intend to enjoy every moment, savor every emotion, release every tear . . .

The crowd cheers again, and the sound of conch shells fill the air. The West Indies have won the toss and decided to bat first.

"Daddy, I want to go to the practice nets," I say, after refusing a drink. Daddy frowns at me and looks over at the nets like they're nylon cages. He hasn't gone back out to fish yet, though the coast guard found *Joanne* rocking against the tide toward the shore, on her way back home.

Just another strange phenomenon in Fairy Vale.

"It's just there," I say, pointing at the nets a few feet away. The Fairy Vale boys are already gathered in the area, probably gushing about which player held their hand on the field.

Daddy nods, and I dart away before he can stop me. I look back and see that he's leaning forward in his seat, stretching to see if I've made it down the steps without dying.

The security guard tries to stop me but Coach Broomes gestures to him to let me come into the area. He knows I've been ill and most likely feels sorry for me. Yeah, I had to get bitten by the poisonous child of a mythical sea spirit for him to be nice to me.

Daddy, Ahkai, and I decided to keep the real truth a secret. We had no proof, and no one would believe us anyway, except Mrs. Edgecombe. She visited me in the hospital a few times—well, "visit" is too strong a word. She would peep into the room to make sure I was still alive, and then hurry away.

Oh, there's also Casper. We told him the whole story at the fish market. He kept staring at the rock, muttering prayers and making the sign of the cross on his chest. A few days ago, Casper—in actual English—whispered that a fisherman claimed he heard sweet singing and loud crying coming from the rock, but people said the guy must have been drunk. But then Casper also told us Elvis stole a jacket from his clothesline that morning, so who knows?

I didn't bother to tell the real story of Daddy's disappearance to Miss Mo. But she did pray for us, and insisted we walk out of the sea backward. No one questioned Mariss's sudden disappearance either, except Ramona, whose belly is growing at an oddly fast pace.

One day, she waddled up our pathway with a bottle of perfume and a loaf of sweet bread for Mariss. She was very upset when we said we didn't have any way to contact her.

I've also not been back to my spot under the silk cotton tree at Coconut Hill. I haven't told anyone about how Mariss came to live at my house, not even Ahkai, but thanks to Miss Mo, I'm not worried.

No one else will be foolish enough to carve into that tree.

I'm enjoying the freedom of swinging at stumps. It's strange . . . Though I've spent the last few weeks in the hospital, my pace seems to be quicker. My sprained knee is as good as new.

It's like it healed itself . . . just like the silk cotton tree. *Just like Mariss.* I shiver at the thought.

"Good ball," says a deep voice behind me. I turn to see Omar Taylor, the Jamaican opening batsman for the West Indies. He's shorter than I expect, with a low afro and black patches under his eyes to help block the sun's glare. Omar smiles at me, and I try to return it, but I can't stop looking at him with a dopey expression.

Omar walks over to the stumps and gets into position. He gestures for me to bowl. Everyone—Coach Broomes, the cricket team, and some spectators—is looking at us.

I focus on the middle stump behind Omar, take a breath, and move to do my run-up. I remember to take an extra four steps back, like Coach Broomes suggested so long ago. I glance over at Coach Broomes. He taps his chin and then puts up one finger.

I take one more step back.

I run toward Omar, who moves his bat up and down, preparing for my ball. He takes a step forward, exposing one of the stumps. I adjust my grip on the ball, changing the angle at the last moment, and release the ball.

Omar swipes at the ball and misses. It knocks the left stump to the ground! Omar looks around at the dislodged stump in disbelief.

Everyone around me starts to cheer, even the crowd! I can hear Daddy shouting, "That's my chile! That's my girl!" and a continuous "Whoop! Whoop!" from Ahkai. A sting of tears comes to my eyes so I pretend to wipe sweat from my forehead with my shirtsleeve.

The Fairy Vale cricket team is applauding, all except Jared, who is pumping his fist and cheering almost as loud as Daddy. I feel my ears burning and my heart does a somersault.

Omar comes over to shake my hand.

"Mi hope sey mi do better 'gainst England," he jokes.

"Is yuh coach dat?" he asks, gesturing toward Coach Broomes. I don't know what to say, so I just nod.

"Coach, yuh ah de boss!" Omar calls to Coach Broomes, and then pats me on the back. "And back straight like arrow. Likkle girl, yuh ah star bowler!"

Omar walks back to the dressing room, swinging his bat. Coach Broomes looks me up and down, tapping his chin. All of a sudden, Jared tosses a ball at me, and as a reflex, I reach out and catch it with one hand.

Coach Broomes shakes his head in a slow, deliberate manner, but then he reaches into a bag and tosses a white-and-blue cricket shirt at me. I catch it and raise it in the air like a prized trophy.

"Finally!" Jared exclaims with a gleam in his eyes. "You've come a long way from hiding behind the tamarind tree."

I realize my mouth is hanging open, and I close it quickly, trying to regain some sort of dignity. But I am so embarrassed, thinking about myself crouching in the grass, trying not to laugh at his silly Ossie Moore jokes. I groan and hide my face with my hand. Jared laughs and turns back to his, I mean *my*, teammates.

I return to Daddy and Ahkai, tossing my new ball into the air.

Daddy is relaxed, legs stretched out and eyes fixed on the field. Ahkai is bopping his head to his favorite imaginary song. Daddy grins at me and kisses me on the forehead when I sit down.

"Vincent! How are you? And Josephine, you look much better!"

It's Miss Alleyne, wearing a maroon West Indies shirt, but with a red flower in her hair. It reminds me of the fresh flowers she brought to my hospital room every week when she came for her physical therapy. She's mostly recovered now, and Fairy Vale Academy has decided to hire her full-time, even though Mr. Atkins is due back next term.

"Hi, Aurora." Daddy smiles, but he doesn't get up from his seat. "Just spending some time with Bean. She been looking forward to this match for a long time."

"Soon we'll be watching *her* from the stands," Miss Alleyne replies, beaming at me.

Before I can answer, the crowd starts to clap. The opening batsmen are coming out from the pavilion. Omar walks backward onto the field before facing front to head to the pitch.

"He's very superstitious!" says Miss Alleyne with a laugh. Daddy, Ahkai, and I exchange a knowing look.

"Well, I better find my seat. See you later!" Miss

Alleyne walks away. Daddy opens his mouth to say something, but then changes his mind. Instead, he kisses my forehead again and takes a sip from his can.

"Miss Alleyne!" I call after her. "Sit with us."

I squash onto the seat with Ahkai, leaving space for her to sit next to Daddy.

Daddy looks at me, eyebrow arched, silently asking the question. I shrug my shoulders. Ahkai's face is still down in the cricket book, but he gives a nod of approval and continues to bop to music in his head.

Miss Alleyne squeezes in beside me.

"Comfortable, Jo?" she asks, looking down at me with a warm smile. She puts her arm around my shoulders and pulls me close.

I rest my head against her arm and get a whiff of her perfume.

Vanilla.

Hmmm . . . it's different, but still nice.

I guess sometimes change can be a good thing.

Acknowledgments

My journey began when I was nine years old and told my cousin that there was a baby trapped under the bed. He was very skeptical, and it took a lot of backstory and character development to convince him. So thank you, cuz (I'm not allowed to name, lest I damage his reputation) for challenging me to tell an authentic story.

Thanks to my mother, Sandra, who went along with my prank, then had to call my auntie to take my scared cousin home. Thanks also to my little sister, Akeeba, who tried to save me when I ventured under the bed to rescue the baby and got "captured" as well.

Of all the books I read in English Literature at school, a short story about a fisherman who became obsessed with a strange mermaid stuck with me, so when I made the rash decision to bang out a first draft in three weeks for a writing competition, Josephine was there waiting for me to tell her story. I want to thank everyone involved in the CODE Burt Award for Caribbean Young Adult Literature, and judges, Karen Lord, Alex Wheatle and Janet Smyth for choosing this story as a finalist and changing the direction of my writing career.

I will be forever grateful to my agent, Marietta Zacker, the fearless literary mermaid who read this manuscript when it was half its size, took a chance on me, and became a tenacious champion for my stories. Thanks also to my fairy god-agent, Erin Casey, who plucked this manuscript out of the slush pile, slammed it onto Marietta's desk, and stared at her until she read the text (this is how I imagine it went down).

Words cannot describe how lucky I am to have an editorial genie like Mallory Kass. Your editorial letters are such gifts, which I plan to frame and hang on my wall. Thank you for being such a fierce advocate for the Fairy Vale crew.

Thanks to the entire Scholastic editorial, sales, publicity, marketing, and production teams, especially Maya Marlette, Josh Berlowitz, and Mary Kate Garmire, who made my manuscript sparkle; Alan Smagler, Elizabeth Whiting, Jackie Rubin, and David Levithan, who were early champions of the work; Lyn Miller-Lachman for her guidance; and the wonderful art director, Keirsten Geise, and too-talented-for-words illustrator, Edge, who made this book more visually stunning than I could ever imagine.

I am not a mushy person, but I have to make an exception for my friends, who believe in me more than I can ever believe in myself. Lloyda gives constant encouragement, and many people (including Lloyda) would be horrified to know I get most of my advice from her.

Every writer, no, every person in the world needs a cheerleader like Liesl. She is embarrassingly supportive, and is known to shame me with her effusive love on social media, whether I win an award or successfully bake a loaf of bread.

Malissa is a bottomless well of support and works logistical magic behind the scenes, just so I can have the space and peace of mind to write.

Special shoutout to Roger Alexis, Ramona Grandison, Gina Aimey-Moss, Shelly Seecharan, Lisa Springer, Sharma Taylor, Ayesha Gibson-Gill, Shakira Haynes, Crystal Chase, Danielle Dottin, Deirdre Dottin, Tanya Batson-Savage, and Joanne C. Hilhouse. This book would not be the same without your encouragement, intelligence, and creative insight.

I also want to thank everyone I forgot to mention. Don't fret; I plan to write many more books so your name will make it into one of these acknowledgments eventually. I appreciate your support in advance.

To Gibbzy, my partner in life, who has been with me on this book's entire journey, and like my own personal Lagahoo, changes into whatever form I need, whether it be arms of comfort, words of encouragement, or a creative wall on which to bounce ideas. In my darkest moments, you are an unwavering source of light.

It is a true blessing that Josephine and Ahkai exist in real life, and they are just as smart, loving, brave, and mischievous as the fictional ones. I can't wait until you both are old enough to read this book. I hope this story brings even half as much joy as you bring to me.

To the aspiring Caribbean author, the world is waiting for your story.

About the Author

Shakirah Bourne is a Bajan author and filmmaker born and based in Barbados. She once shot a movie scene in a cave with bats during an earthquake, but is too scared to watch horror movies. She enjoys exploring old graveyards, daydreaming, and eating mangoes. Learn more at shakirahbourne.com.